She needed evidence

And the attic was the place to look. Wasn't that where all the detectives she'd seen and read about always went?

Caitlin mounted the stairs, picturing her stepfather up there plotting with his gang of cut-throat murderers.

The room was dark, and she stood ready for something, someone, to jump out at her. But nothing stirred. When she bathed the room in light from the overhead fixture, she spied an old trunk. In it were only old magazines, yellowed with age. But what was that, way down . . . ?

A wooden box. Locked with some kind of weird puzzle. Caitlin fiddled with it and grinned when the lid popped open. Nothing but a bunch of papers inside.

She picked one up, smoothed it out, her eyes getting bigger and bigger. There was her name, written in bold ink. Caitlin Ashley Emerson had hit the jackpot.

ABOUT THE AUTHOR

Heather McCann is thrilled that her first book sale is to Intrigue. Writing a romantic mystery, according to Heather, combines the best of both fields. When asked how she got the idea for *The Master Detective*, she replied, "A devious mind is a rare and wonderful thing. Ideas come from everywhere—chance conversations, newspapers, magazines and meeting strangers. All one has to do is keep a receptive mind and a sense of humor!"

The Master Detective

Heather McCann

Harlequin Books

TORONTO • NEW YORK • LONDON
AMSTERDAM • PARIS • SYDNEY • HAMBURG
STOCKHOLM • ATHENS • TOKYO • MILAN
MADRID • WARSAW • BUDAPEST • AUCKLAND

To the Ladies' Monthly Sewing Circle and their generous and wise advice and counsel. And also to Chris, without whose expertise, Caitlin wouldn't have seen the light of day.

Harlequin Intrigue edition published December 1992

ISBN 0-373-22207-6

THE MASTER DETECTIVE

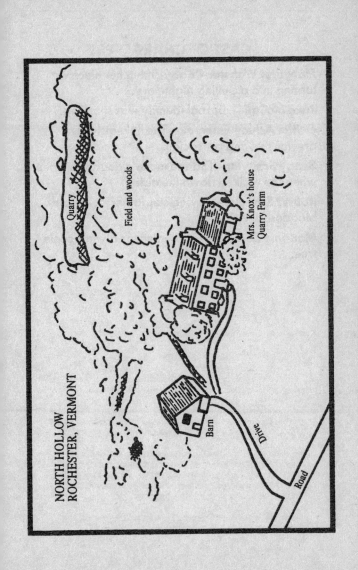

NORTH HOLLOW
ROCHESTER, VERMONT

Quarry

Field and woods

Mrs. Knox's house
Quarry Farm

Barn

Drive

Road

CAST OF CHARACTERS

Margaret Webster—Baby-sitting her niece was turning into a chilling nightmare.

Jake McCall—His real identity was shocking.

Caitlin Ashley Emerson—The little girl was precious . . . and precocious.

Sandy Schuyler—Did she make a deadly mistake when she walked down the aisle?

Robert Schuyler—Loving stepfather . . . or cold-blooded killer?

Madame Zorina—Her predictions always came true.

Chapter One

Seven-year-old Caitlin Ashley Emerson knew a secret nobody else knew. She hitched her long, purple dress up higher as she crept upstairs. The dress was her mom's. Sunglasses, a red felt hat and glittery fairy wings completed her ensemble. It looked as if she was playing dress up, but she wasn't. Caitlin was wearing a disguise. Master detectives did that sometimes.

Her disguise had been thought through carefully. First she'd tried on her mom's red high heels, but the shoes made too much noise. The whole idea was quiet stealth, after all.

She was determined not to get caught. The hard part was getting past the front hall without being seen, and she'd already done that.

She heard soft noises from downstairs and stiffened against the wall, her heart banging against her ribs. Then there was a squeak, like sofa springs shifting, someone getting up and walking across the rug.

Fear filled her inside, making it hard to breathe. She took a deep breath and began humming an old nursery rhyme. Softly, barely a whisper. "'A B C, tumble-down D. Cat's in the cupboard and can't see me.'"

They couldn't see her.

The murmur of adult voices came from the living room, and the sudden sinister sound of footsteps approached. She ducked down and flattened herself against the wall again. As she held her breath, the footsteps stopped, then the front door opened and closed. She let out a breath of relief. Someone had gone out. Her stepfather, no doubt. He'd probably gone out to start the car. Robert and her mom were flying to Florida, and he wouldn't want to miss their plane. A sense of injustice crept over her. It just wasn't *fair.* Why should they get to go to Florida and see Disneyworld, and she couldn't? No, she had to stay behind in this stupid old rented house in Rochester, Vermont, baby-sat by her Aunt Margaret for two whole weeks. Stuck up here on top of North Hollow, which was sort of a small mountain. Her mom had explained all the dumb, grown-up reasons she couldn't go with them. But Caitlin hadn't been fooled. This was all Robert's idea. Maybe her mom was tricked, but Caitlin could see through him. He didn't want her along.

Phooey. She didn't want to go anywhere with him, anyway.

She hitched up her dress again, conscious of a burst of feminine laughter downstairs. Her mom and Aunt Margaret. They were too busy talking to bother looking for her, but she waited, anyway. Master detectives had to be prepared for the unexpected.

Nothing happened. Then, assuming a limp for the benefit of anyone who might be observing her, because that's what master detectives would do, she made her way up the rest of the stairs, only to stumble slightly just as she neared the top.

The murmur of voices from the living room stopped. Her mother came into the hall. "Caitlin, are you all right? What happened?"

She turned as her mother hurried upstairs. "I'm okay. I tripped on my dress, that's all."

"How many times have I told you to be careful when you play dress up? Honestly, that dress is a menace." Sandy slid a comforting arm around her daughter's shoulders and kissed her cheek. "The stairs are steep, honey. You could take quite a tumble. Be careful, and promise me you'll be good for Aunt Margaret while Robert and I are gone."

"Okay."

Her mother gave her another hug. "Robert and I are leaving now. Are you coming out to the car to say goodbye?"

Caitlin frowned and shook her head vehemently underneath the red felt hat. "No."

"Honey, it's only for two weeks. I'll miss you." Caitlin tightened her mouth. Her mother sighed. "I wish you'd try harder to like Robert. He likes you very much."

Only a fool would think Robert really liked her. Grown-ups who liked kids didn't hog all the dessert so no one else could get seconds. And they didn't pinch you when no one was looking.

She looked up at her mother and said, "I don't want to go out to the car, Mom. I'm really busy... playing. I'm going to give my Barbie dolls a shampoo."

"All right," Sandy said, giving up at last. "Give me a kiss goodbye. I'll call you from Florida when the plane lands." She straightened Caitlin's fairy wings. "There, that's better. I love you."

Caitlin reached up and slid her arms around her mother's neck, kissing her cheek. "I love you, Mom. Bye."

"Bye, darling." Her mother gave her another kiss and hug and went downstairs. After a few moments the sounds of adult conversation resumed from the living room, and Caitlin breathed a sigh of relief and went down the hall to the little sewing room, which she wasn't supposed to enter. Well, so what? Her Mom wasn't even going to be here. She was going to Florida, leaving Caitlin behind.

She went inside and closed the door quietly, her trained eye missing nothing. Detectives had to notice and remember little details. She looked around, aware of everything. There on the table by the window, together with the blue and white china lamp and the heart-shaped brass box with no peppermint candy in it because she'd eaten the last piece, propped against the alarm clock, was a photograph of herself. It had been taken about six months ago, right after her mother's marriage to Robert. Caitlin had been dressed in jeans and her red Mickey Mouse sweater. She'd been holding a teddy bear. In the picture Robert had his arm around her shoulder, his hand resting on the teddy bear's head. Wind had blown her tawny brown hair, and she was smiling, her two front teeth on the bottom missing.

Thoughtfully, Caitlin sucked on her lower lip. Those two teeth were almost in now, but one of her front teeth on top was missing and the other one was loose. Well, that meant another fifty cents from the Tooth Fairy. And if she kept her room clean for a week or two she'd have enough allowance for more Barbie clothes.

She looked across the room toward the half-open window. At the front walk she could see Robert loading up the trunk of the car. Mr. Perfect. He sure had her mom fooled. A sudden spring breeze blew the curtain in and out. It fluttered into a shaft of weak sunlight, nubby gold threads in the cloth shining all glittery. It was like an omen that everything would be okay, and the master detective would find what she was looking for. Clues.

She bent down and looked under the green-checked sofa. Nothing but little curls of dust up by the wall and the edge of the rag rug. She turned her attention to the closet, but it held nothing but the landlady's winter jackets and suits and a big, bulky parka with a fur collar. She closed the closet door with a sense of disappointment. Where else would a detective look? There had to be *something*.

A small desk stood near the sofa. Working with the skill of a cardsharper, she slid the drawers open silently, one by one. Nothing but sewing magazines and patterns. Carefully she felt the underside of the drawers, just as she'd seen the Bloodhound Gang do it on TV, when they'd investigated the secret of the Martian's curse. Her fingers met only smooth, cold metal. Then, as she felt beneath the middle drawer, she touched something else . . . paper.

She knelt down, her face level with the middle drawer, and she could see it. A small snapshot taped to the bottom of the drawer. Her small fingers worked at the tape, and at last she managed to peel most of it off. The snapshot only tore a little as she pulled it free.

She closed the drawer and looked at it. The top left corner was missing, but that couldn't be helped. She sighed. It wasn't much, just a dumb picture of a man with a mustache, but it was a start. She put the snapshot in the pocket of her dress just as the front door opened downstairs.

There was a short laughing conversation, then thudding feet running up the stairs. Heavy, masculine feet. Heart pounding, she ran to the door and was just closing it behind her when Robert reached the upstairs landing.

His eyes flickered toward the doorknob. He knew she'd been in the little sewing room. She hadn't been quick enough.

He smiled, blue eyes twinkling, pretending he wasn't mad at her. "What are you up to, sweetie? Playing?"

She fixed the sunglasses that were sliding down her nose. "Yes."

He paused a second, glancing again at the door, then said, "Almost forgot the airplane tickets. Your mom would have been furious if we'd gone all the way to Montpelier Airport and had to come back." Half-laughing, he shook his head and went into their bedroom. A few seconds later he came out and went downstairs, calling over his shoulder, "Bye, Cait. See you in a few weeks." Pausing by the front door he went on, "Sandy, it's late. Better shake a leg."

Upstairs, Caitlin turned and went into her bedroom. Kneeling by her bed, she felt around underneath for the hidden shoebox. She put the snapshot inside, then slid the shoebox back underneath the bed and went to give her Barbie dolls a shampoo. Not that they really needed it. It was an ingenious diversion designed to confuse the watchers who might have penetrated her disguise.

DOWN IN THE LIVING ROOM Sandy Schuyler was looking distractedly through her purse. "God, I'd lose my head if it weren't fastened. Where's that key?"

Margaret smiled widely. "You already gave me the front door key, if that's what you're looking for."

Sisters, different as night and day. Margaret Webster's shoulder-length hair was black as a raven's wing, her eyes, green as the sea, while Sandy was fair and blue-eyed. In their twenties, both were energetic and pretty, although Sandy was now pale and thin.

Sandy picked up her purse and walked toward the front door as Margaret opened it. They embraced in a warm hug. "I'm so glad you agreed to watch Caitlin and the house while we're gone," Sandy said. "I really... well, I thought maybe you wouldn't come."

Margaret's green eyes crinkled with warm affection. "Why wouldn't I come when my big sister calls?"

"It's awkward, that's all. Robert and I've only been married six months, and well..." Shrugging, Sandy twisted her purse strap between her thin fingers. "I thought maybe you still had feelings for him. Oh, I know I should have known better." She half laughed and hugged Margaret again. "I've been such a fool. What you and Robert had at one time wasn't love."

"Of course it wasn't, silly," Margaret lied. "Now hurry up and get to the airport or you'll miss the plane. Everything will be just fine here. Don't worry."

Sandy frowned. "Oh, I almost forgot. Since this house is rented, it's full of the landlady's things. Mrs.

Knox left the house as is, when she went to Europe. I told Caitlin not to touch anything that didn't belong to us. Actually, I put the fear of God into her, she's so stubborn. I told her the landlady was a cross between Freddie Kreuger and the Wicked Witch of the West. Lord knows if it's enough to keep her out of the poor woman's belongings.'' Her mouth quirked into a smile. "Caitlin reminds me of you when we were kids. Always up to something, full of make-believe. I swear, half the time she can't tell the difference between what's real and what isn't. Remember when you were seven and took that swan dive off the shed roof with the towel pinned to your back? You were sure you could fly.''

Margaret nodded ruefully. "I broke my ankle and wore a cast half the summer. I missed out on all the swimming, and it itched like crazy.''

Outside, a car door slammed. A breeze blew in through the half-opened door, and spring sunlight spilled across the faded Oriental scatter rugs on the wood floor. Sandy glanced at her watch and said, "Oh dear, I'd better go.'' She leaned over and kissed Margaret's cheek, then dashed down the front porch steps and out to the car.

Margaret waved to Robert from the porch. She didn't want any physical contact with him. "Bye, take care of Sandy.''

He glanced up at Margaret, smiling. "See you in a few weeks, Maggie. Take care.''

He was the only one who'd ever called her Maggie. For a moment she relived the last time they'd been alone together, that summer night one year ago. She could feel again the warm, humid, night air as they'd sat in Robert's car, parked outside her Boston apartment house on Marlborough Street. He'd reached for her. "Maggie, I'm so sorry, but Sandy and I are in love. It just happened—one of those things. I've asked her to marry me. Dammit, I didn't want to hurt you, but there's just no other way. What we had wasn't real. Someday you'll realize I'm right. There's someone else for you, darling . . . a better man than I'll ever be."

His handsome face with its heavy eyebrows and mobile mouth had been drawn and pleading. The roof light had snapped on as she'd wrenched the door open and slid out of the car. Running blindly across the sidewalk and up the steps, she'd prayed she would get inside before she broke down.

She took a deep breath. Dammit, that terrible night had happened a year ago. It was over and done with. A whirlwind romance that had fallen apart. She'd only dated Robert for a few months before their short-lived engagement. Then he'd met Sandy at the home of mutual friends, and that had been that.

She swallowed back a rush of hot tears. She'd worked hard to change, this past year, letting her cropped black hair grow until it lay in tangled curls to her shoulders. She reached up and pushed back her hair and seemed to hear an echo of his laughing voice.

God, it still hurt so. She wiped her face with the back of her hand, then waved as their car edged down the drive. She stood a moment, watching as the car turned and disappeared down the road.

The view from the house was breathtaking. Huge twin maples flanked the front walk. Beyond, about thirty acres of open hayfield sloped down the valley to distant blue mountains on the far side of the White

River. A hilly patchwork of hayfields and meadows were dotted with black and white cows and sheep. Peaceful. The river glittered in the distance, a silver ribbon winding along the valley floor. Ethereal tendrils of mist floated above the water, quiet and still. Only the caws of blackbirds disturbed the silence. Drawing a deep breath, she relaxed as a sense of serenity and healing washed over her. Life went on. There were other men in the world besides Robert. All she had to do was wait. Sooner or later he would turn up, and she would be drawn to him....

A gentle breeze wafted the fragrance of an immense clump of lilacs that grew by the porch steps.

It was going to be a wonderful two weeks. Laughing softly, Margaret stepped back inside the house and closed the door.

The pine grandfather clock chimed from across the front hall. Eleven o'clock—and somewhere in the house water was running.

She frowned and listened. It sounded as if it was coming from the upstairs bathroom.

It was. Caitlin was calmly shampooing her dolls' hair—and water was overflowing the sink. There must have been at least a half inch of water all over the floor. "I'm shampooing my Barbies," Caitlin said, watching her aunt get down on her knees to mop the floor.

A half dozen dolls in various stages of wet dishabille smiled vacantly at her from the confines of the overflowing sink. "Turn off the faucets, please," Margaret told her niece. "Didn't you notice the water was overflowing? Mrs. Knox owns this house and wouldn't like it if the floor fell apart, which is what happens when it gets soaked." She glanced at Caitlin who stared back with heart-shaped sunglasses perched on her head. Her eyes were deceptively innocent.

Caitlin opened her mouth and said calmly, "I forgot about the water. Anyway, you're not the boss of me. I can do whatever I want."

Margaret let that remark alone. Time enough to sort out who was in charge of whom around here. First things first. She wrung out another sopping towel in the tub and mopped under the sink. Caitlin got off the toilet seat and stood on the end of the towel. "How come your hair is black? I mean, Mom's is blond. Did you dye your hair?"

"No, and move your foot, please—no, Caitlin, the one you're standing on the towel with. And don't touch that bottle of shampoo." Margaret closed her eyes as the bottle fell on the tile floor.

Caitlin gathered up her dolls and headed for the door, throwing Margaret a challenging look over her fairy wings. "I'm hungry, and I'm allowed to eat whatever I want, 'specially popsicles."

"I doubt that," Margaret said to her departing back. "Wait a minute. I'll get this cleaned up, then I'll make us lunch." Caitlin shouted something that sounded suspiciously like 'I hate lunch,' and Margaret mopped as fast as she could. Five minutes later she raced to the kitchen and found her niece busy making flour and water paste for glue. The sink, countertops, everything was glop, including Caitlin, who was indignant when Margaret washed her face and hands.

"I like being dirty," she said belligerently, making a hideous face.

Margaret finished cleaning Caitlin's face. "Now I can see who you are again." She dropped a kiss on her niece's freckled little nose. "Know what? I love freckles."

"I hate them," Caitlin muttered. "And I hate Robert, too. Why didn't they take me to Florida. It's not *fair*."

"Because your mom's been sick, and the doctor said she needed plenty of rest and sunshine so she'll get better."

Caitlin put her sunglasses on and said, "Robert's mean. He pinched me."

By this time Margaret was slathering whole-wheat bread with peanut butter and grape jam. She screwed the top back on the peanut butter and said, "I know Robert pretty well, and I don't think he's mean."

"That's because he didn't pinch you. He pinched me," Caitlin said. "I want a popsicle."

"After you have lunch." Margaret gave her a level look. "And I mean it. Lunch first."

"I hate whole-wheat bread. Those weird brown bits are bugs," Caitlin announced, jutting her firm little chin. "I'm not eating any bugs."

"They're not bugs."

"I don't care. I'm not eating it."

Hoping to divert Caitlin's attention long enough for her to forget the brown specks in her sandwich, Margaret picked up a Barbie. The doll was wearing a wedding dress and missing an arm. "What happened to this one?"

Caitlin shrugged her fairy wings. "Her arm got falled off. It's a 'bomination. That's what happens when doctors take parts of you off. Like if you're crazy they take your head off and fix your brain. Then they stick it back on."

Margaret cleared her throat, then managed to say, "Where did you hear this?"

"Mrs. Till, the lady who comes to clean the house, was talking on the phone in the kitchen, and I came in to get a drink. I didn't listen on purpose. It's kind of comp'cated. She poured me some milk and kept on talking to this friend of hers named Ruth Ann. She said it was a 'bomination that killed old Mr. Knox after his first wife, Martha, died . . . and he must have been crazy to fall for Polly Knox." Caitlin leaned across the table and said confidentially from behind her heart-shaped glasses, "'There's no fool like an old fool.' That's what Mrs. Till said. She said Polly had him roped and tied before he knew what hit him. Polly was Martha Knox's nurse. Martha was sick and old, like Mr. Wendell Knox. She didn't have a 'bomination, just a heart attack what killed her dead."

"I see," Margaret said, trying and failing to get all this straight.

Caitlin took the one-armed Barbie from Margaret's nerveless fingers and inspected it clinically. "I prob'ly shouldn't play with her until I get her arm stuck back on. Maybe it's in the bathroom. I'm gonna go look." She slid off her chair and ran out of the kitchen.

Margaret made a cup of coffee and sat down to catch her breath. Caitlin was a holy terror. Give her an inch and she'd take a mile.

Half-listening for the sounds of water running, Margaret closed her eyes and slipped off her shoes. It had been a whirlwind two days, finishing up everything at the office so she could take a few weeks off and come to Vermont to help Sandy out. Her boss had been understanding, even kidding her about sneaking off to get in some spring skiing.

Fat chance. There wasn't any snow left, and forsythia and lilac were already in bloom. Tulips and daffodils, too. Sandy had picked her up, and once they'd driven over the White River Bridge and turned toward town, it seemed spring had suddenly announced itself. She smiled, remembering one house in particular... about a quarter mile past the bridge. Victorian, white, with spires, a big front porch with a bay window, and of all things, a bright green parrot on a perch in the window. There'd been a woman in the window, feeding the parrot a cracker. She'd had the brightest orange hair. A sign swung in the wind on a post in front of the house: Madame Zorina, Palm Reading, by Appointment Only.

CAITLIN WAS BACK from the bathroom and busily soaking her sandwich in her milk when Margaret opened her eyes and came out of her reverie. "How come I couldn't stay with my dad while Mom and Robert were in Florida?" she wanted to know.

Margaret sighed and fished the pink, mushy remains of lunch out of the glass, in the process spilling most of it. She started mopping up and explained, "Because your dad's in Europe right now." Frank Emerson, Sandy's first husband, owned a small computer company. His dedication to business was the reason their marriage had collapsed. He had had no time for his daughter, either.

Margaret looked across the table at Caitlin who was eyeing the freezer speculatively. She had to smile. It wasn't hard to figure out what was on her niece's mind.

Abruptly, Caitlin said, "How come this house is called Quarry Farm? What does *quarry* mean?"

"A big hole in the ground. Your mom says there's a marble quarry in the field behind the barn."

Caitlin frowned, not looking very interested.

"The quarry in the back field is flooded, honey. It's full of water, at least three hundred feet deep. You're to stay away from it unless I'm with you." Margaret gave her a look, wondering if any of this was getting through. She couldn't read any expression behind those heart-shaped dark glasses.

"I can swim," Caitlin said after a moment. There was something about the innocent tone of her voice that told Margaret her niece wasn't a great swimmer.

"Really."

"Yes." Caitlin looked at her over the top of her glasses. "Do you believe me?"

"Sure, if you say so," Margaret said, smiling blandly and making a mental note to watch her like a hawk around any water.

The front doorbell rang loudly, and Caitlin jumped off her chair and ran down the hall yelling, "I'll get it." Margaret hurried after her in time to see her let in a stout, gray-haired woman carrying a shopping bag of cleaning supplies.

The woman smiled and removed a blue silk scarf from her hair. "Hello, you must be Mrs. Schuyler's sister from Boston. I'm Louisa Till, the housekeeper. I come in and help out once a week."

Margaret shook her hand. "Yes, you have no idea how glad I am to see you."

"Like I say, I come in once a week. Caitlin, honey, stop pokin' at that lace." The housekeeper unbuttoned her cardigan sweater, put down her shopping bag and gently swatted Caitlin away from the fragile lace panels by the front door. "I swear, if there's somethin' somebody doesn't want a child to get at, it's just what they go for. Must be some sort of magnetism. I got five of my own, grown now, thank the Good Lord, but they were all like that, every last one of 'em. Enough to drive a person batty." She turned to Caitlin and said, "Run and play now, that's a good girl."

After mulling this over a moment, Caitlin wandered off to the living room and lifted the piano lid with a crash. Loud discordant banging ensued. "Stop foolin' 'round with Mrs. Knox's piano," Mrs. Till shouted. She looked at Margaret and shook her head. "Lord! Well, I'll be gettin' on with my work. The kitchen floor needs a waxin'." She glanced down the hall toward the living room. The banging hadn't stopped, but had slowed and gentled, clearly becoming some sort of tune.

"I'm practicing," Caitlin yelled belligerently from the piano bench as she launched into scales. "Mom says I have to practice an hour every day."

"Oh, no," Margaret muttered with a groan.

"Maybe I'll vacuum, instead," Louisa said wryly, and turned and bustled off to the kitchen, shopping bag of cleaning things in hand.

Margaret went upstairs to get her purse, after which she pried Caitlin away from the piano and told her to change into jeans and a sweater for a ride to Rochester. She found Louisa vacuuming the back hall, and shouted over the vacuum's roar, "I need to get milk and eggs. Caitlin used the eggs and milk in a 'scientific experiment.'" Louisa rolled her eyes, and Margaret just smiled.

After Caitlin was finally ready, they went to the garage. Robert's little black Fiat Spyder was there—the same car they'd been in when he'd broken off their engagement. They got in, and Margaret coaxed the battery to life. Robert had told her that the battery was weak and the brakes might need adjusting. He was still the same, expecting cars to run without maintenance. Margaret thought it was about time he became more responsible, especially since Caitlin had to ride in his car.

She let out an angry breath of frustration as the engine sputtered and finally caught with a deafening roar. Cautiously she backed down the drive and headed toward town. The dirt road was rutted, narrow and steep, requiring all her concentration. It wasn't until they'd almost reached the bottom of the mountain that she noticed Caitlin was very busy writing something in a notebook. She was humming what sounded like "Twinkle, Twinkle, Little Star," and her head was bent over her work. One small hand held a corner of the notebook while the pencil formed somewhat squiggly words.

It looked like a list of some sort.

Margaret flipped the turn signal and pulled out on Route 100, heading toward town. "What are you writing?" she asked after a moment.

Caitlin gave her a suspicious look, then said firmly, "It's a secret. Very comp'cated. I'm not telling, and you can't make me."

"Who said I was going to make you?"

"Well, you can't, that's all. And you can't be mean to me, either. That's against the law."

Margaret pushed back her hair, and her mouth quirked. "I have no intention of being mean to you. I love you, silly." She looked over at her niece, and the suspicious expression in Caitlin's wide, innocent, blue eyes touched her with a small jolt. Unconsciously she straightened a little.

Caitlin bent her head again, scribbled something, then said, "How do you spell *gold digger*?"

A little shocked over Caitlin's question, Margaret glanced at the notebook, then looked back at the road. They'd reached the center of Rochester. There was a big, white church on the left side of the green. Something was going on . . . a church fair. Cars were everywhere. The green was full of tents and booths. She noticed a popcorn cart, flea-market tables and even a fortune-teller's booth. Maybe Caitlin would enjoy having her fortune told.

"I *said* how do you spell *gold digger*?" Caitlin frowned in annoyance.

The supermarket was just ahead. Margaret pulled the car over to the curb and turned off the engine. "*G-o-l-d d-i-g-g-e-r.* Why do you want to know?"

Quickly Caitlin closed the notebook. "I *told* you, it's a secret. Very comp'cated and *important*."

Chapter Two

In the fortune-teller's tent on the green, Madame Zorina sat alone. She was a fat woman with abundant hair dyed a garish orange. Sometimes she consulted the Ouija, sometimes her pendulum, a glass crystal suspended on a cotton thread.. She had great ability with both, but right now she was laying out the Tarot.

She'd shuffled the cards over and over, but they still came out the same. She tried again, sliding the cards together, her rings glittering in the dim, murky light. The Death card came out on top. Death, cloaked and riding a pale horse. She covered it with the Queen of Wands.

Her brother, Vern Boyce, came in with a folding chair. She gathered up the cards and put them away as he began to string a curtain of colored beads across the tent doorway. He whacked a nail crookedly into the tent pole, looped the beads across it and climbed off the chair. He'd been drinking since early morning, and by now he was, as usual, well oiled. He stuffed the hammer in his belt, jerked his head at the beads and snarled, "Yer all set. I'll be back 'round five. I'll be needin' some money."

Madame Zorina reared back from the cloud of bourbon emanating from her swaying brother. Stooped and graying, his face tanned and seamed with wrinkles, he glared at her. "All right," she said grudgingly. "But you lay off that booze. We'd have a chance at getting ahead on some of the bills if you'd stay sober."

He leaned toward her, his rheumy blue eyes blazing like flames. "Mind yer own damn business. I got somethin' goin' that'll mean big money. Somethin' you don' know nothin' about."

"Oh?" she said casually, straightening the paisley cloth covering the card table. There was a crystal ball on the table along with her deck of Tarot cards. "It'd make a nice change if you brought home some honest money."

The air in the tent was strangely golden and murky; sunlight shafted dimly through its canvas sides. A gust of wind rattled the beads, and Vern turned to leave. He hesitated a second, then said, "D'ya see anythin' about me today?" She looked across the table, staring right through him, seeing something past him in her mind. She nodded, and he pulled up the chair and sat down. "Tell me what ya saw. Was it money?"

She shook her head and said slowly, "Your aura is...dull and leaden. Be careful, Vern. I don't know what you're up to, but it's not going to turn out right. I used the pendulum this morning, and I saw terrible black fog enveloping you. It's a warning."

Sweat beads started prickling his face. He stared strangely, hypnotically, mumbling something. "Look, I'm going to get more money than you've ever seen in yer life," he said gruffly. "A real big score. I can't stop now. Ahh nuts, yer bluffin!"

Madame Zorina stood quite still. "I had visions. I saw things. There was an evil woman—with murder in her heart. And another woman with black hair and green eyes. She was with a child. Their coming will mean terrible trouble."

He lurched out of the chair, tossing it over with a clatter. "I don' know nobody like that. Yer crazy, just like the doctors said."

"Greed means death. Things are not what they seem." Her voice was a low, guttural rasp.

Blindly he began backing away. Sweat ran down his back. "Give up a chance of a lifetime to get big money?" He laughed loudly. "Over my dead body."

IN THE CEREAL AISLE of the supermarket, Caitlin intently examined the back of one brightly colored box. "Hmm, this looks good." Actually, she'd never tried this cereal, and really only wanted the orange yo-yo prize inside. She eyed her aunt thoughtfully, wondering if she knew sugared cereal was supposed to be bad for you. Maybe she didn't know about Mr. Tooth Decay and kids getting hyper on sugared foods.

Margaret turned from inspecting different brands of tea bags and noticed Caitlin stuffing the cereal in the cart on top of the bag of oranges. "Are you allowed to eat that?"

"Sure." Caitlin looked down at her purple sweater and yawned. "Besides, I'm wearing purple. That means I'm the queen and get anything I want."

"No kidding."

"Yes." Caitlin smiled with satisfaction. "I'm gonna be queen all the time and tell everyone what to do. Queens get to sit by kings, and everyone has to bow down to them. I think it's real neat."

Due to Caitlin's missing tooth, all her *s*s sounded like *th*s. Picking up the cereal, Margaret exchanged it for one that looked more nourishing. "Let's try corn flakes, instead."

"I hate corn flakes. Queens don't eat them." Caitlin's eyes shot daggers at the box in question. "I want the one with the yo-yo inside."

"Not today. Even queens don't get their way all the time." Margaret pushed the cart up the aisle toward the dairy section. Caitlin followed, grumbling that it wasn't fair, and that queens did, too, get their way, otherwise what was the point of being queen?

"Maybe it's better just being yourself," Margaret suggested, putting a half gallon of milk and a dozen eggs in the cart.

"I can be myself any old time," Caitlin sniffed. "I want to be somebody else besides."

"Like queen of the world?"

Caitlin didn't smile. Where her wants and desires were concerned she had very little sense of humor.

They went through the checkout, and Margaret only had to tell Caitlin twice to put candy back.

"But why? Mom lets me have candy."

"I'll bet. Once in a blue moon." Margaret pushed the loaded cart through the door and outside. "Look, there's a country fair on the green. Want to go?"

Caitlin grinned, her eyes brimming with excitement.

Margaret put the grocery bags in the backseat of the car and locked it. Then they headed to the green.

"I *love* cotton candy. Can I play all the games?" Caitlin asked as they approached the fair.

"I don't see why not. Which booth do you want to try first?"

"Gosh, I don't know." Caitlin crinkled her nose. "I think I'll try the fishing one, but first I want some cotton candy." She grabbed Margaret's arm and dragged her to the food stand.

Caitlin satisfied her sweet tooth, then played a few games, winning two prizes, a cardboard monkey that jumped up a stick when its string was pulled, and a huge peppermint lollipop. They strolled past the fortune-teller's tent, and Caitlin aimed straight for it. "Let's go in here. I want my fortune told. Does she really know the future?"

Margaret's eyes twinkled as she pushed aside the bead curtain in the booth doorway. "Not really, but it's fun. And it's for a good cause. The church is raising money for a new roof."

The glittering beads rattled shut behind them, and Madame Zorina looked up from her crystal ball. Around her neck she wore a bandanna scarf sewn with gold coins. A black, flowing, glittering gown hung from her ample shoulders. The tent was airless, the lighting dim, yet Margaret realized the fortune-teller was the same woman she'd noticed in the house by the bridge. Her hair was the same odd shade of orange, piled high in mounds and coils, fixed with tortoise-shell pins.

Feeling a little embarrassed, she moved forward and said, "We wanted our fortunes told. Do you use the crystal ball?"

Madame Zorina stared hard at Margaret for a long moment, then said, "I read palms for two dollars. The crystal ball costs more."

"Oooh neat! I want her to read my palm," Caitlin declared, hopping up and down with excitement.

"The lady first," Madame Zorina said, gesturing to the chair across the table. "Then I will read yours."

Margaret sat down and put a five-dollar bill on the table. She took a deep breath and extended her hand, palm up. The fortune-teller's dark, glowing eyes fixed on her hand.

"Your name is...Margaret," Madame Zorina said slowly.

"Why, yes, that's right," Margaret said, staring at the woman, astonished. For some reason she shivered a little. There was something eerie about the way the woman was looking at her.

Behind her chair Caitlin whispered a mystified "Wow, how'd she know that?"

Madame Zorina began tracing a line across Margaret's palm. Her finger trembled slightly, and her breath made a hissing sound. She spoke again in a strange, dull voice. "You have been very unhappy. It is here in your palm. You have loved and lost. But now...another man will enter your life and change it forever."

Caitlin whispered loudly, "What does that mean?"

Madame Zorina raised her strange glowing eyes and said, "It means nothing will be the same. There is more here. I see great danger. Not for you, lady, but for another."

"Oh, really," Margaret laughed, half-embarrassed. She started to get to her feet, but the fortune-teller grasped her wrist, preventing her from standing.

"I was wrong. You are in danger, too," she hissed. "You must be careful. Beware of the silver serpent. The time of danger approaches with the full moon."

Finally Margaret managed to wrest her arm free. "Thank you, I'll be very careful." She stood and told Caitlin they were leaving. "It looks like it might rain. I'd like to get back home before it starts."

"What about my fortune?" Caitlin sat down in the chair. "I don't want to leave yet."

"All right," Margaret said with a sigh.

Madame Zorina took Caitlin's hand and peered into it for a moment. Then she frowned and said, "You are young. There's little here to see." Her voice trembled and her face shone with perspiration.

Caitlin stuck out her hand again. "It's not fair! I paid my money. I should get my fortune."

Reluctantly Madame Zorina looked at her palm again. "You will be a catalyst. You will make the difference between life and death for one whose life hangs in the balance." Abruptly she stopped speaking and dropped Caitlin's hand. Fumbling amid the folds of her black gown, she made the sign of the cross. "Here, take back your money. It's not fitting. Go...go!" She made flapping motions with her hands, all but shooing them out of the tent.

"What happened?" Bewildered, Caitlin stared at Margaret as they stumbled through the curtain. "How come she told us to leave?"

"I don't know." Margaret paused and slid a gentle arm around her niece's shoulders. "Never mind. Let's get something to eat. Aren't you hungry? I am!" She steered them both across the grass toward the hot dog concession stand. She realized that the fortune-teller had been badly frightened. Stark fear had lurked in her eyes. Whatever she'd seen in Caitlin's hand had scared her to death.

Shrugging mentally, Margaret decided not to worry about it. They were at a country church fair to have fun, not to dwell on ridiculous dark warnings from some woman dressed in exotic beads and bangles pretending to foretell the future.

Reaching the concession booth, they bought two hot dogs with the works and two sodas, then wandered over to a nearby maple tree and sat down to eat. Caitlin had trouble disentangling the paper wrapper from her hot dog. Most of the mustard and relish ended up down the front of her bright purple sweater.

"Want some help?" Margaret said offhandedly as another blob of mustard plopped into Caitlin's lap.

"I can do it myself. I'm not a baby!" Caitlin chewed in silence for a while, then burst out with "How come I didn't get my whole fortune! I got cheated! It's not fair!"

Lips curving in a smile, Margaret glanced at her niece. "The fortune-teller gave the money back, so you really got your palm read for free."

"Sure, but you got a whole fortune. I only got half."

"Well, I'm twice as big as you are, so my fortune's bound to be twice as long." Margaret didn't have much hope in Caitlin's buying this feeble argument, and she was right. Her niece looked at her with scorn.

"That's dumb. I got cheated, I know I did. She got to the part where I was going to do something important, and she just stopped! How come she didn't tell me everything?"

"Madame Zorina's pretty old." Margaret screwed up her hot dog wrapper and picked up the napkins Caitlin had strewn all over the grass. "Maybe she was tired and couldn't read any more palms today."

Caitlin gave her an intent look. "Hmm, you're pretty old, and she's got to be even older 'n you. Maybe she took a nap and she's rested up now. Why don't we go back?"

Ignoring the remark about her being "pretty old," Margaret looked across the green toward the fortune-telling booth. "Madame Zorina's gone. Her booth's closed."

"I WANT TO SEE a movie," Caitlin demanded loudly. She yanked Margaret's sleeve. They were walking past the town movie theater just as a matinee was starting.

Margaret looked at the poster by the ticket booth. The movie seemed suitable for kids. "Okay, I guess we can go." She bought tickets, and they went inside. Luckily the show was just starting. Caitlin sauntered down the aisle and picked a row about twenty feet from the screen. She sat down, leaving the end seat for Margaret.

Caitlin crammed some popcorn in her mouth. "The ending's kind of dumb, but I like the part where the spaceship lands in the shopping mall." She chomped another mouthful and looked at two little girls who sat down next to her.

Margaret frowned. "You've already seen it?" Caitlin nodded through a handful of popcorn, and Margaret said exasperatedly, "Why didn't you say so?"

Caitlin shrugged. "I felt like seeing it again."

The little girl next to Caitlin whispered something in hushed conversation. Margaret glanced around the near empty theater deciding they weren't bothering anyone. And after all, it would do Caitlin good to talk to someone her own age. Life had to be lonely for her up on the mountain. There were few close neighbors, let alone any with children.

Margaret settled back in her seat and watched the movie. Every once in a while she caught a word or two of Caitlin's whispered conversation. The other child said her name was Nancy and she had two brothers and a cat called Tiger because of his stripes.

"Where do you live?" the little girl asked between bites of her candy bar.

"In Mrs. Knox's house," Caitlin whispered loudly. "We're renting it. My mom got married to Robert, and we moved here last month."

Nancy stared curiously at Caitlin. "The *Knox* place?" Caitlin nodded and Nancy chewed thoughtfully on her candy bar. "Mrs. Knox married old Wendell for his money, and he died. She got plenty. My mom says she's set for life and she's blowing a mint on that trip to Europe she's taking."

The other little girl, whose name was Kelly, leaned over and said, "Yeah, my mom says Mrs. Knox has more money than a dog has fleas. Is your family rich, too?"

Caitlin shrugged. "Mom inherited money from some old aunt last year, but Robert's just got his job. He works for some drug company, he sells stuff to doctors and hospitals." She frowned and asked in a low voice, "What's Mrs. Knox like? Is she weird, or what?"

"Kind of stuck-up." Kelly unwrapped a chocolate bar. "Want some?"

"Sure." Caitlin broke off a piece and put it in her mouth. She chewed a minute, then turned and said to Margaret, "I'm thirsty. Can I get a soda and a candy bar?"

All three little girls were looking at her hopefully, so Margaret took a few dollars from her purse and handed it to Caitlin. "Be sure and come right back." Immediately all three girls ran up the aisle, giggling and whispering.

Left alone, Margaret watched the screen without really following the movie. She thought about the bizarre fortune-teller. It was odd that Madame Zorina had known her name. Well, there could be a logical explanation. Maybe the town grapevine was working overtime. People knew everybody's business in a small town like Rochester.

Margaret frowned, remembering that the woman had known about her unhappy love life. But most women had their hearts bruised once or twice by the time they were in their mid-twenties. That had been standard fortune-telling patter. The other things Madame Zorina had said about danger coming with the full moon, false lovers, the silver serpent was non-sense.

Margaret drew a deep breath and let it out again. Madame Zorina should have known better than to scare a small child with talk of death.

The three children came back and pushed past Margaret into the row. "Oh, here's the best part," Caitlin pointed out in a loud voice. Immediately a woman sitting two rows toward the back of the theater told her to be quiet. Caitlin scrunched down in her seat and grumbled, "I only said it was the best part."

The scolding seemed to have an effect; for a short time all three girls watched the movie in comparative silence. Only the crunch of popcorn and slurp of soda interrupted the dim quiet of the theater. But once action erupted on the screen, Caitlin leaned over and began whispering to Nancy and Kelly again. Every once in a while Margaret heard Mrs. Knox's name mentioned, so she tapped Caitlin on the shoulder.

"Stop talking. You're ruining the movie for everyone else."

Caitlin shrugged, stuffing the last of her popcorn in her mouth. "This is the most boringest part, anyway."

"I don't care. Other people want to watch it. Now be quiet."

With a loud sigh, Caitlin settled down in her seat. When the movie ended a few minutes later and the lights came up, Nancy and Kelly ran up the aisle after yelling goodbye. Caitlin walked just ahead of Margaret, balancing a half-empty soda and three candy bars.

"Caitlin," Margaret said as they came out into the street and moved through the straggling crowd. "Gossip isn't nice. You shouldn't have talked about Mrs. Knox to those little girls. How would you like it if people talked about you behind your back?"

Caitlin tossed her head. "I wouldn't care. Besides, I'm going to be a detective or maybe a writer when I grow up. They have to know practically everything, and how can you find out things unless you ask questions?"

Margaret didn't have an answer for that. She unlocked the car and told her niece to get in and fasten her seat belt.

They drove to a nearby station to get gas. There was a car at the self-serve pump. A tall, dark-haired man had just finished and was hooking the nozzle back on the pump. He was handsome in a craggy-faced way, and Margaret felt a little unsettled when he glanced at her. The fortune-teller's prediction floated through her mind. She wouldn't become obsessed over every good-looking man she saw.

When they got back to the farm, Louisa was just leaving. She beeped her horn and drove off down the road. Parking in front of the big red barn Margaret unloaded the groceries.

"Can I play outside for a while?" Caitlin asked, looking at her aunt with puppy eyes.

"Okay." Margaret picked up the last bag and closed the car door. "But don't go far. It looks like it might rain."

The sky to the west was darkening. Rolling clouds topped the mountains in the distance, and a brisk wind had sprung up. It smelled like rain, and the mountains were now indigo, except in their shadowed folds, where they looked almost black.

Deciding she would give Caitlin twenty minutes or so to play outside, Margaret closed the door and went to the kitchen to put away the groceries.

CAITLIN MADE a beeline for the door at the side of the barn. She'd tried it yesterday, and it had been open. Nothing much to see inside but musty old hay and a bunch of rusty tools. But she'd noticed a canoe paddle by the hayloft. That might have interesting possibilities.

The door creaked as she pulled it open. She went inside. In the utter stillness of the barn's dim interior, her footsteps sounded loud. The only light came from dusty windows set high in the barn walls. She hesitated a moment, hearing a soft scurrying sound from a nearby stall. Mice, prob'ly. She wasn't scared of mice. Well, not much, anyway.

Swallowing hard, she looked to the left, toward the hayloft. The paddle was still there. She picked it up and ran back to the door, closing it behind her.

There was a barely perceptible path leading up through the weedy field. Carrying the paddle, Caitlin made her way up the path through the field to the top of the slope. On the other side of the field, surrounded by woods, lay the quarry. Dark green stone lined the steep sides. Birch and pine saplings grew in cracks of the stone, and she could see that the path continued downward, curving around to the south side of the quarry, emerging far below near a large, flat slab of marble.

A small wooden boat was tied up by the large rock. It was perfectly obvious the paddle belonged to the boat. What would be wrong with taking the boat out for a while? It was Mrs. Knox's, and she was in Europe. She wouldn't care, Margaret thought happily.

She shifted the paddle to her left hand and grabbed on to a birch sapling as she made her way, slipping and sliding down the quarry path. She knew she should ask permission to use the boat. But that would be dumb. If she didn't ask, she couldn't be told no.

Wind rustled in the trees as she reached the large rock on the far side. A few raindrops began to fall, but by now she was determined to take the boat out for a ride. She untied the rope and got in, clutching the side of the boat for balance. It wobbled, and she sat down on the seat in the middle and paddled away from the rock.

She grinned. This was really neat, really fun.

She took a look at the far side of the quarry. It seemed a long way away. Leaning over, she peered down into the green water. It was clear and looked about a thousand miles deep. She could see way down past the dripping paddle, where the water changed imperceptibly from green to black.

Caitlin dipped her fingers in. It was cold—and deep. She wondered what kind of fish swam in the quarry. Dolphins? No, they lived in the ocean. Sharks probably...or deep-sea monsters lurking down in the depths. Maybe she'd got her fingers out just in time. What if they surged up and knocked the boat over? She would die, her body sinking down to the bottom...unless sea monsters swallowed people whole.

She was being silly and took a deep, reassuring breath. Sharks lived in the ocean, also. And there would only be small fish, like the ones that nipped her toes last summer in the pond in the town where they used to live before her mom married Robert.

Caitlin paddled some more, and the boat swung out toward the center of the quarry. Overhead, gray clouds massed, their shadows racing over the water. She felt their chill for a few moments before they raced on, leaving sudden shafts of sunlight so brilliant that the shadows cast by the trees lining the walls of the quarry looked black as ink. Imperceptibly the errant raindrops grew harder, and thunder rumbled in the distance.

MARGARET WAS just folding up the last of the grocery bags when the doorbell rang. She went to open the front door and found a tall, dark-haired man standing on the front step. He smiled warmly, and Margaret guessed he was in his early thirties. "I was looking for Robert Schuyler. My name is Jake McCall."

A little shiver of excitement ran down her backbone. He was the same man she'd seen at the gas station. He topped six foot three, with thick black hair brushed back casually from his forehead, tanned skin and a hint of crow's feet at the corners of his gray eyes. Warm appreciation lurked in his smile. Though large and rugged-looking, there was an odd gentleness about him.

Releasing the breath she'd unconsciously been holding, Margaret said, "Robert's away at the moment. Are you a friend of his?"

His gaze flickered from her sneakered feet up her jeans past her fire-brigade-red sweater to her slightly flushed face. ''Yes, I'm an old friend. Actually, I'm his former brother-in-law. He was married to my sister, Betsy.''

Chapter Three

"Please, come in," she stammered, her mind in a whirl. He held out his hand as she closed the door. As his fingers gripped hers she felt a tingling sensation all the way up her arm. "I'm ... well, it's rather complicated. I'm Margaret Webster, Robert's sister-in-law."

They moved into the living room as she explained about Sandy's having married Robert the summer before. Jake nodded and said, "I heard he'd married again. I haven't seen him since...well, in some time." And he sat down in a wing chair.

Margaret sat on a small Hepplewhite settee as the clock in the hall chimed six. She said with a puzzled frown, "I can't get over Robert's having been married before. He never mentioned it. I can't understand why—were he and your sister divorced?"

Jake hesitated for a second. His quick smile faded as he unbuttoned his tweed jacket. "No, my sister died suddenly three years ago. I was out of the country at the time. I'm a civil engineer, and my job sometimes takes me abroad." There was a small silence, then he went on, his voice lower, "Robert was with her when she died."

"I'm so sorry," she said inadequately.

"Betsy had asthma and a heart condition, but medication had kept it under control for years." His voice rasped and he cleared his throat. "My family was in shock when she became ill...and then suddenly died."

Margaret felt very uncomfortable and was caught off guard when Jake asked, "I gather your sister and Robert are happy?"

"Of...course," she stammered, "they couldn't be happier. They've gone to Florida for a couple of weeks." The words just seemed to continue as she added, "Sandy's been sick, some sort of flu. Her doctor suggested rest and warm weather to prevent pneumonia from setting in. I'm taking care of my niece, Sandy's daughter from her first marriage." When he didn't say anything, Margaret added, "Caitlin's seven, and a holy terror."

He studied her for a long moment. "You look like you can handle her."

"Sometimes I'm not so sure," she said. Then, feeling awkward again, she continued, "How did you find out where Sandy and Robert were living?"

"Believe me, it wasn't easy. When I got back from Australia, Robert had sold the house and moved out of town. He and my sister owned a place in Connecticut." Jake shrugged his wide shoulders. "It's pretty involved, and I got lucky. The people who bought the house remembered Robert's saying at the closing that he'd changed jobs. He mentioned a possible move to northern New England. I knew he was crazy about skiing. We'd always talked about it, and he described Rochester, a quiet town west of Rutland where he'd spent some time skiing. I had to come north on business and took a chance he might have ended up here. A few calls downtown at the local realtors, and I hit paydirt."

"I see," she said with a small smile.

"Robert's a great guy. I didn't want to let the family connection drop."

"Yes, he's pretty wonderful," she agreed, the distant, pain-filled expression in her wide green eyes telling Jake she was hiding something.

He'd damn well touched a nerve there, he knew. Her face was pale now, leaving her pensive looking. Her generous mouth was set in a determined line, as if she'd made up her mind about something. But just as quickly as he'd caught her expression of sadness, it was gone, and he wondered if he'd imagined it.

"Do you live in Vermont ordinarily?" He shot her a curious look.

The clock chimed six-fifteen, and she glanced toward the hall with a frown. "No, I live in Boston. Sandy and I grew up in western Massachusetts. This is my first visit to Vermont. It's so quiet and peaceful." Abruptly she rose from the settee. "I'm getting a little nervous. My niece is playing outside, and I really ought to check and see if she's all right. There's a quarry up behind the barn. I told her to stay away from it, but with Caitlin you never know."

"Why don't I go with you?" he suggested easily, getting to his feet.

Margaret was already down the hall. She yanked open the back door and called Caitlin's name. When there was no answer she ran outside, past the red barn with its dark, staring windows, then up through the field, blackberry canes whipping at her jeans.

The wind was rising, gusting, and rain spattered against her face. Thunder roared and crackled beyond the smoky blue of the clouds massed over the mountains.

"Caitlin?" she yelled again and again above the wind. The night was dark and wild, the sky eerily lit with streaks of yellow lightning to the west.

"Caitlin?" Jake McCall's voice boomed behind and to her right. Still no answer. They kept running, plunging through the scrubby undergrowth toward the steep edge of the quarry.

And suddenly there was Caitlin, sitting in a small boat, paddling madly toward the quarry's edge. The boat appeared to be making some headway, although it wobbled furiously from side to side.

"Oh, God," Margaret cried. Cupping her hands around her mouth she yelled, "Caitlin, make for shore. I'm coming!"

Jake came up behind her and caught her arm. "Let me go first. I'll get her."

The last thing she wanted was an argument, and anyway, Jake could probably reach Caitlin sooner. She nodded quickly, following him down the steep path, frantically grabbing saplings to keep from falling. Already he was several yards ahead, running as he neared the bottom of the path. When he reached the flat rock, he dove in and swam out toward Caitlin in the wooden boat, which by now was going around in circles.

Dragging in a shaky breath, Margaret ran the last few yards to the rock. Rain was pouring down in sheets; she could hardly see the boat with Caitlin in it.

Lightning flickered, eerie and blue. Then suddenly the quarry lit up bright as day, and she saw them clearly. Jake had hold of the prow of the boat and was determinedly swimming back toward shore.

Over the rumble of thunder he yelled, "*Sit down,* Caitlin. I'll take you in!"

For once Caitlin did as she was told, although there was a mutinous expression on her face.

When they reached the rock, Margaret helped her out of the boat and hugged her. "My God, I'm glad you're all right!"

Jake climbed up on the rock and tied the boat's mooring line to a sapling. "It was a close call. That's no place to be in a rainstorm."

Caitlin frowned, hunching her small, wet shoulders. "I was only doing Mrs. Knox a favor."

"I'll bet." Margaret grabbed her arm and marched her back up the path to the top of the quarry. "I told you to stay away from this place. What possessed you to come down here?"

"Mrs. Knox left the boat out. I was just going out for a little ride before taking it back to the barn. Mom says to put stuff away when you're through with it, so I thought I'd—"

Margaret hustled her along through the blackberry bushes. "Not another word. I don't want to hear any of it. You're taking a bath and going straight to bed when we get back to the house." She turned her head and called to Jake who was bringing up the rear with the paddle. "Would you lock that up in the barn, please?"

"Sure," he said and headed diagonally through the field toward the barn.

Caitlin was still complaining nonstop. "I can swim, honest. You can ask Mom when she calls. She'll tell you it's okay if I go to the quarry by myself."

By this time they'd reached the back door. Margaret ushered Caitlin inside. "I don't care if your mom says you swim the English Channel every six weeks! You're not to go near that quarry while I'm responsible for you, and that's final!"

A large puddle of water was accumulating around Caitlin's small, sneakered feet. She sneezed. "It's not fair. I never have any fun anymore."

Margaret dragged Caitlin upstairs to the bathroom to take a nice hot bath. Over her niece's objections, she helped her off with her sodden purple sweater. And as she unsnapped the button of Caitlin's jeans, Margaret half listened for the slam of the back door. Jake was taking a long time putting the paddle in the barn.

As if she'd been reading Margaret's mind, Caitlin sneezed again and said suddenly, "Who was that man who pulled me out of the water?"

"A friend of Robert's," Margaret muttered as the back door slammed. Caitlin kicked off her sneakers, then yanked off her socks and threw them in a heap on the floor. Margaret sighed tiredly and said, "Pick up your things and put them in the hamper."

Ignoring this, Caitlin climbed into the tub. "Robert used to know Mrs. Knox, too, a long time ago."

"Where did you hear that?" Margaret remembered Sandy and Robert talking about the landlady. They said they'd only seen the woman once, when they'd signed the rental agreement at the realty office down in Rochester.

"I read a letter he wrote to her. He signed it, 'love.'" Caitlin lay back and began kicking her feet, making violent waves that slopped over the sides of the tub.

"Stop that. Where did you find a letter from Robert to Mrs. Knox?" Margaret stared at her niece, forgetting completely that she'd told her over and over it wasn't nice to pry into other people's affairs.

Sitting up, Caitlin began soaping her rosy-pink belly. "I'm not telling. It's a secret." She threw a sidelong glance at her aunt. "Want to play riddles? I'm really good at it."

Margaret opened the cabinet door and rummaged around for shampoo. "Okay. You start."

"Long neck, crooked thighs, little head and no eyes. What am I?"

Thinking hard, Margaret picked up the shampoo, closed the door and turned back to the tub. Caitlin was scrubbing away at the bottom of her left foot.

She frowned as Margaret knelt by the tub and took the top off the shampoo. "Don't get that stuff in my eyes. It stings. Come on, what am I?"

"I won't, I promise. And I don't know." Margaret poured a little in her hands and began sudsing Caitlin's already wet head.

"A pair of fire tongs! I told you I was good! Want to play again?"

"No, I know when I'm out of my league." After rinsing Caitlin's hair, she helped her out of the tub and toweled her off. "Wrap that around you and get into your pajamas."

Caitlin nodded, then looked up and said, "Know what Nancy said?"

"Nancy?" Margaret's brow furrowed slightly, and then she remembered the little girl in the movie theater. "Okay, I remember her now."

"Her mom says Mrs. Polly Knox has a lot of nerve. After old Wendell Knox died, even before the grass was green on his grave, she had a man move in." Caitlin tilted her head. "How long does it take for grass to get green?"

"I don't know." Margaret leaned down and let the water run out of the tub. "Where did you hear this nonsense?"

"You never listen. I told you, Nancy's mom. She said there was this big scandal. Polly Knox told everyone that the man was her cousin, but nobody believed it. Nancy's mom says Mrs. Knox wouldn't know the truth if it walked up and bit her on the ankle, and that her supposed cousin was shiftless and bone lazy. What's *bone lazy* mean? How can your bones be lazy?"

Margaret sighed with exasperation. "They can't, but they can get tired. Maybe this cousin of Mrs. Knox's was sick, but that's not the point. This is gossip, and you shouldn't listen to it. Whether or not Mrs. Knox's cousin came to stay at her house is none of our business. When Nancy started talking about it you should have changed the subject."

Caitlin looked at her in stubborn silence. Then she burst out, "Mrs. Knox and her cousin fought a lot about money, too." The expression on her face said that she knew this for a fact.

Margaret gave her a long, serious look. "How do you know they did?"

"I'm not telling. Anyhow, it's a secret." Caitlin hitched the towel up under her arms as if that were the end of the discussion.

Unfortunately Margaret knew that Caitlin's enormous bump of curiosity had been aroused as far as Mrs. Knox was concerned. She'd poke her nose into every nook and cranny of the poor woman's life, and nothing would stop her.

Launching into a lecture about leaving other people's things alone, about trust and the violation of privacy, Margaret stopped in mid-sentence and asked, "Do you understand what I mean, Caitlin?"

"No."

"Do you care?"

"No. I *told* you I'm going to be a writer or a detective when I grow up. Writers have to find out stuff."

Margaret gave up. "Go get your pajamas on, then blow-dry your hair. The dryer's in the closet on the middle shelf. You do know how to use it?"

Caitlin nodded and turned toward the door. She took a step, then looked over her shoulder. "Mrs. Knox left her winter coats in the sewing room closet, but the one in her bedroom has lots of uniforms in it. White ones. She used to be a nurse." There was a secretive smile on her face.

Margaret drew a deep breath, emphasizing every word as she spoke. "No more going into her bedroom. It's off-limits."

"Mom told me there was a law passed so you could find out stuff—the Freedom of Information Act." The tone of Caitlin's voice was superior, implying it was too bad her Aunt Margaret was so dumb.

"That law has nothing to do with snooping in that woman's bedroom closet. You stay out of her room, and I mean it!"

Caitlin tossed her head and went to her bedroom while Margaret went downstairs to the kitchen. Jake was at the stove, just turning the gas on under the kettle.

"I hope you don't mind, but after that soaking, I thought we could both do with a hot cup of tea." He grinned, his hair dark and wet with quarry water. In fact, he was wet from head to foot.

Margaret sighed. "I'm sorry. I forgot you were soaked, too. Let me get you a towel from the downstairs bathroom."

His grin widened. "I could use one."

A minute later she was back with a thick blue towel. He took it and scrubbed furiously at his hair, wiping his face and neck as the kettle whistled.

Margaret switched the gas off and got down two mugs. "I can't thank you enough for your help."

"How is Caitlin? No ill effects, I hope." Jake's deep voice held concern.

"No, she's fine. She went off to get her pajamas after lecturing me on the Freedom of Information Act. Honestly, she's only seven, but she'd try the patience of a saint."

He raised an amused eyebrow. "An only child?" She nodded, and he said, "That explains it."

Margaret got out tea bags and poured boiling water in the mugs. "There's cream and sugar on the table, or I can get you lemon if you prefer."

He pulled out a chair for her. "No, this is fine." His hand brushed against her back as she sat down, leaving a trail of warmth. He sat across the table and stirred sugar into his mug of tea. "Does it worry you, staying here alone while your sister's away?"

She shrugged. "At first I didn't give it much thought. But now I realize it's quite a responsibility. This place is full of valuable antiques. I pray that Caitlin doesn't break anything."

His eyes caught and held hers. Gray blue, magnetic, darkly lashed, with those laugh lines at the corners. Nice eyes, direct, honest. They were smiling at her, saying he liked what he saw.

He sipped his tea and lowered the mug. "The landlady must have insurance if she's renting."

"I hope so. She'll need it," Margaret said grimly. She sat back in her chair with a sigh. "The truth is, I'm not concerned so much with what Caitlin breaks. It's everything else she does that worries me. Every time I turn around she's poking her nose into Mrs. Knox's belongings or eavesdropping on conversations. She's even got a notebook she carries around with her, writing down everything she hears. Her excuse is that she's going to be a detective or a writer when she grows up. And they need to know everything. That's where the Freedom of Information Act comes in. She's decided it gives her carte blanche."

He laughed, a relaxed, easygoing laugh that brought a smile to her lips. "What else does Caitlin do?"

"She practices the piano every day for an hour. I'd like to lock it up and throw away the key—she's that bad."

"I remember my piano lessons when I was about that age." He smiled and scrubbed his hair again with the corner of the towel. "The metronome ticking away. Pure torture. I don't know how my teacher stood it. On a good day I'd hit one note in ten. And I didn't have many good days." He leaned back in the chair and went on musingly, "Poor old Mrs. Perkins probably wore earplugs. Either that or she was deaf as a post. Taught piano to generations of kids. A real martinet. Once I hid a grass snake in the piano and sat there, figuring she'd call the lesson off when she found it."

Margaret sat back in her chair, unable to contain the beginnings of a grin. "What happened?"

He shrugged. "Mrs. Perkins had the last laugh. She picked up that snake and threw it into her garden without turning a hair, then kept me practicing scales for an extra half hour. She was really something else. They don't make characters like that anymore."

"I wonder." Margaret ran a thoughtful forefinger up and down the handle of her mug of tea. "I met a woman today who was quite a...character. A fortune-teller down at the church fair on the town green."

"Sounds interesting," he replied with a distinct twinkle in his eyes. "What happened?"

She took a sip of tea. "Caitlin and I saw her sign, Madame Zorina, Famous Psychic—Palms Read for Two Dollars. So, we went inside. Everything seemed fine." She paused a moment in recollection. "No, that's not true. She seemed upset as soon as we entered the tent. Maybe it was my imagination working overtime but she seemed to turn white as a sheet the minute she laid eyes on us. And once she began reading our palms it got worse.''

''What happened?''

''At first she said the usual thing, that I'd meet a tall, dark-haired stranger who would change my life.'' Margaret threw him a slow, shy, half smile. ''I guess you'd qualify.''

''Ahh, the plot thickens,'' he drawled teasingly. ''What else did she predict?''

Margaret gave an embarrassed laugh. ''Oddly enough, she knew my name and something else about me.'' She hesitated a second, then explained, ''The truth is Robert and I were engaged for a short while before he met my sister. He fell in love with her, and that was that, as they say. It was mainly bruised pride, but at the time . . .''

There was a little silence, then he said quietly, ''It felt like your heart was broken.''

She gave an embarrassed shrug, realizing suddenly with a dawning feeling of surprise that she was finally over Robert. He was simply someone she'd loved once. That terrible aching hole in her heart was gone for good, and with its passing she felt a lightness inside. An incredible sense of freedom.

She lifted the mug to her lips and said self-consciously, ''I didn't mean to bore you with a rehashing of my love life. It's odd, though. Madame Zorina put her finger on it just like that.''

''Probably a lucky guess.''

''Two lucky guesses?'' she said, trying to sound nonchalant, as if the fortune-teller hadn't actually frightened her.

"What else did she say?" His face was solemn, concerned, with just a trace of a lingering smile in the curve of his mouth.

"There was terrible danger ahead, for me and someone close to me. Something about a snake and a full moon." She shrugged uneasily. "I know it sounds crazy, but there was an eeriness about her I can't explain. Her eyes looked...almost transparent, not just glowing, but lighted from within. Like a Halloween pumpkin." She gave a little shudder and went on. "Maybe it was the tent. It was so dark you could hardly see your hand in front of your face. And while she was telling our fortunes, I...I really believed her."

"She might have a little ESP, but it sounds as if she's just a typical con artist," he said thoughtfully.

Margaret leaned forward. "When she started reading Caitlin's palm she got frightened for some reason and wouldn't tell us what she saw. Her hands were shaking." She drew a breath and said, "Naturally, Caitlin wouldn't leave until she had her fortune told. Finally Madame Zorina gave in. She said Caitlin would be a catalyst and make a difference between life and death in someone's life. Then she gave us back our money and threw us out of the tent. She even made the sign of the cross. I almost felt like Dracula!"

"No trace of fangs from where I sit," he said with a grin, gray-blue eyes dancing. "Madame Zorina's got quite a line in hokum."

She sat back and tugged her sweater down slightly. She wished she'd been more particular about what she'd packed in the way of clothing. The red sweater, although her favorite, soft and warm, was three years old and getting shabby and thin in spots. She tugged at the hem of the sweater again as she noticed Jake's gaze flicker over her shoulders and lower.

"Sorry to be such a mess. I wasn't expecting company. Living way up here, Caitlin and I dress more or less to please ourselves."

His eyes strayed from her creamy smooth face and heavy mane of curly hair to her gently rounded slenderness. "Don't mind me. I don't count as company. Just your garden-variety brother-in-law, once removed." A hint of laughter threaded his deep, husky voice.

Feeling a wave of warmth that had nothing to do with the hot tea she'd been drinking, she fiddled with her teaspoon. The trouble was he didn't look like any garden-variety brother-in-law she'd ever seen. Even one once removed. He was too darned handsome.

Dark, rugged good looks, lean athletic build and an easy, engaging smile, reflected in eyes the color of the evening sky. She drew a deep breath, deciding he was nice enough. He hadn't displayed any wolfish tendencies, although she'd noticed his eyes looking her up and down.

"Vermont's beautiful, isn't it," he commented after a moment. "There's a sense of peace that's indescribable. You went so quiet on me there, I thought maybe you'd fallen asleep."

She smiled and shook her head. "Not asleep, maybe dozing a little, though. The peace of mind creeps up and takes you by surprise. When I first arrived, I was still running at the usual stressed-out level. But after I'd been here a couple of hours I noticed how calm I was. I'd love to find a small place up here when I'm drawing social security."

"Somehow, when the time comes, I doubt you'll have to count on social security for subsistence," he said with a wry grin. "I expect there'll be a long line of men who'll offer you a good deal more than that."

She gave him a level look across the table. "That's supposing I'm in the market for some man to support me, which, I assure you, I'm not."

"A case of once burned, twice shy?"

"Perhaps. I prefer to call it common-sense independence. I like standing on my own two feet. It's something I've been doing a long time. My parents died my last year in college. Except for Sandy, I've been more or less on my own ever since."

"Independence is fine, but living up here on the mountain you'd better make damn sure the car's in working order."

She gave a little laugh. "Now that you mention it..."

"What?"

"It's Robert's car. The starter sticks, half the time third gear doesn't work, and the battery's temperamental."

He got up. "I'm pretty good with engines. Why don't I take a look at it for you?"

"That'd be great." She smiled gratefully and went with him to the back door. "It's out by the barn. Here's the key."

"No problem." He pocketed the key and opened the door. Wind blew in droplets of rain. "Be back in a minute." With a flash of a smile he was gone, running toward the barn.

JAKE OPENED the driver's door of the Fiat and leaned in to pull the hood latch. It jumped in his hand as he felt the hood pop open. The interior of the car smelled of wet leather and something else, faint and flowery...like Margaret he thought. Getting in, he tried the starter. It turned over reluctantly. The dashboard battery light flickered and died—so did the engine.

He tried again, flooring the accelerator. This time the engine caught, hiccuped once or twice, then settled into a low roar.

The car needed a tune-up, for sure. He pulled the parking brake. It felt loose. He got out and looked under the hood, poking around at the plugs.

He pulled one out. Corroded as hell. He put it back. Just like Robert. Never kept a damn thing in running order.

He used a handkerchief to wipe grease off his hands and got back behind the wheel. The engine wasn't running like a top. If he had tools and parts, he would replace the plugs and wires himself.

Leaning down, he switched off the engine and pocketed the key. He sat there a moment longer, watching rain run down the windshield. His attention was caught by a shining drop of water running along the inside seal. A leak. Rain continued dripping, thudding monotonously on the floor mat on the passenger side.

Something shiny winked at the edge of the mat.

He leaned past the gearshift and pulled back the mat, his fingertips touching something glittery and hard. He picked it up. An earring. Little diamond chips surrounding a red, oval stone. He frowned. It looked like a ruby set in platinum. Expensive. Maybe Margaret's or her sister's.

He got out and slammed the door. Head ducked low against the rain, he ran back to the house and up the steps. Margaret looked disconcerted when he dropped the earring in her palm and told her where he'd found it.

"Well—it must be Sandy's. It's not mine. I'll tell her you found it when she calls."

"If there are tools in the barn, I'll fix the car. It needs a tune-up, and the brake cable's snapped."

She drew in a deep breath. "I don't want to put you to any trouble. I'll get it fixed at the garage in town."

He smiled at her. "You don't want to drive that car. Especially with Caitlin in it."

He could tell from the firm set of her chin that she hated to ask for favors. Her answer was indirect. "No, I don't want to take a chance and break down."

He grinned. "Tell you what. I'm tired now, but tomorrow I'll fix the car, and we can go out to dinner. How's that?"

Her green eyes met his, looking mildly amused. "If you're suggesting a night out on the town, I accept."

"Great." He turned to leave. "If there's an emergency before I get it tuned up, be careful."

"I will."

She walked him to the front door, and when he reached his car, he glanced back at the house. Shivering, she thought of Madame Zorina and her predictions.

UPSTAIRS, Caitlin peered over the stair banister for a moment, listening. Nothing but the low murmur of voices coming from the kitchen. They would be busy for a while, she thought hopefully. Time to do some more detecting, like Sherlock Holmes. She frowned. Aunt Margaret had said Mrs. Knox's room was off limits. Surely the Freedom of Information Act applied in this case. If a person really needed to find out stuff, then it'd be okay to snoop. It'd practically be their duty to go investigating.

Mrs. Knox's room was just down the hall. Pushing it open, she went inside and looked around. Blue and white wallpaper with flowers on it, a big canopy bed and a dressing table with a mirror.

If there was one thing Caitlin liked, it was mirrors. She went over and sat on the bench in front of the dressing table, looking admiringly at her reflection. She turned her head sideways and glanced at her profile. She practiced a few smiles.

Growing bored, she looked down, noticing there was a drawer in the dressing table. She pulled it open. A tube of lipstick rolled sideways in the drawer, coming to a stop next to a photograph half-hidden by a box of face powder.

This was more like it, she thought happily. Face powder and lipstick! Prying the lid off the box, she discovered to her delight that it contained a fuzzy pink puff. She dabbed some powder on her cheeks and nose, gazing critically in the mirror. Maybe lipstick would look good. She took the top off the tube and leaned close to the mirror, concentrating with all her might as she colored her lips.

It was hard to do. The orchid-pink tube slid sideways off her upper lip, garishly marking her cheek.

Some got on her nose, and she used tissues to get most of it off.

She stared at her reflection and decided she needed another layer of lipstick. There! Now she looked beautiful. Replacing the tube in the drawer, she picked up the photograph. It was boring. Just a woman with blond hair in a pink, frilly blouse. A big tree with lights and decorations could be seen behind the woman, and she held a half-unwrapped box in her hands.

Losing interest, Caitlin dropped the picture back in the drawer and slid off the bench. Just then she heard the sound of the front door closing downstairs. She tiptoed out into the hallway and looked around. No one was upstairs. That meant Aunt Margaret was someplace downstairs. What if she came upstairs? If Aunt Margaret found out she'd been in Mrs. Knox's room, she'd probably be punished. Well, she would say she'd just forgot. That was an excuse that worked pretty well, most of the time.

She went into the bathroom, deciding to blow-dry her hair. Even Sherlock Holmes prob'ly dried his hair once in a while.

As Caitlin had predicted, Aunt Margaret came upstairs, walked into the bathroom, took one look at her face and groaned. "Oh, no! Where'd you get that lipstick? It's all over your face!"

Chapter Four

Caitlin cast a dreamy look at her reflection in the bathroom mirror, admiring the way her mouth glimmered. "It's only a little smeared. I got it practically all off. Aren't I pretty? I look just like Barbie."

Margaret was too busy soaping up a facecloth to answer immediately. But as soon as she began scrubbing, she had plenty to say. "Never mind *Barbie*. How *could* you?" She drew in an angry breath. "I told you over and over to stay away from Mrs. Knox's bedroom. That's where you got the lipstick, isn't it?"

Caitlin eyed her aunt, wondering exactly what tone to take. Even under the diffuse lighting of the bathroom she could detect the flush rising on her aunt's throat, could see the grim line of her mouth. She was real mad.

"I forgot."

Aunt Margaret's mouth got madder looking. Without a word she turned and went down the hall to Mrs. Knox's bedroom. Caitlin took one more look in the mirror, then trailed after her. "I didn't hurt anything."

But Aunt Margaret apparently didn't care that she hadn't broken anything. She was busily cleaning lipstick smears off the top of the dressing table and throwing away littered tissues.

Caitlin yawned and wandered over by the dressing table. It only took a second to pull open the drawer. "Look what I found. A Christmas picture." She held it up, and Aunt Margaret took it from her fingers, barely glancing at it before tossing it back in the drawer. Caitlin picked up the lipstick. "How come Mrs. Knox left this behind when she went away? It's brand new."

"How should I know? She must have more than one lipstick. Maybe she got tired of that shade of pink." Aunt Margaret looked around the room for a moment, then marched Caitlin out into the hall and shut the door firmly behind them. "I'm going to make pizza for supper. Do you think you can behave for half an hour?"

Caitlin looked at her aunt with mild amazement. What was she talking about..."behave." Of course she could do that. "Sure."

Aunt Margaret's reaction was interesting. The look on her face registered frustration, irritation and a sort of hopeless resignation. In Caitlin's experience, grown-ups generally reacted like that, even when you weren't actually breaking anything. She waited for a long, boring lecture.

It didn't come. Instead, Aunt Margaret gave her a thoughtful look, then patted her shoulder. "Okay, I'll put the pizza in the oven. Then we can watch a movie. There're some tapes in the den."

"I know how to run the VCR. Mom lets me."

Another thoughtful look, then Aunt Margaret smiled. "Find a movie you like while I get supper ready."

She turned and went downstairs to the kitchen. Caitlin waited until the coast was clear, then climbed onto the banister and slid downstairs.

Sherlock Holmes was still on the job.

It took only a minute to put *Escape to Witch Mountain* in the VCR and turn it on. Aunt Margaret wouldn't complain about a movie like that, and it was loud enough to cover up what she planned to do. Searching the den prob'ly wouldn't make a lot of noise, but master detectives didn't take unnecessary chances.

Tall bookshelves ran along the far wall of the den. A lot of books with hardly any pictures, Caitlin thought, surveying the brightly colored spines. Still, there might be a clue, something written in invisible ink or in secret code. She smiled in pleasurable anticipation. No problem for Sherlock Holmes, hot on the trail of a master criminal. An open-and-shut case.

She dragged the piano bench over to the bookshelves.

MARGARET SLID the pizza into the oven and closed the door. She savored a minute or two of relative peace and quiet, if one could call the movie sound track floating down the hall from the den soothing.

Placing napkins and plates on the table, Margaret froze when she heard a thump and a sharp cry of pain. That hadn't sounded like a movie. She dropped the napkins on the table and ran to the den.

Sure enough, Caitlin was just picking herself up from the floor. Obviously she'd fallen off the piano bench. She rubbed her small backside. "Ouch."

Margaret helped her up. "Are you okay?"

Caitlin nodded. "Uh-huh. I just fell off the bench."

"I thought you were going to watch a movie."

Caitlin turned away and stuffed something white into her pajama pocket. "I am, in a minute. I was looking for a pencil. For my notebook writing. I broke the point on this one. See?" She turned around and held out her notebook and pencil.

Margaret frowned. Something funny was going on. Caitlin hadn't been holding that pencil a minute ago. No, there'd been something white in her hand. It had looked like a folded piece of paper.

Caitlin was wearing her round-eyed innocent look. Margaret sighed and said, "There's a sharpener in the kitchen. I'll sharpen it for you."

Shrugging, Caitlin flopped on the sofa and began watching the movie. "Okay. Let me know when the pizza's ready. I'm starved."

With a frustrated shake of her head, Margaret went back to the kitchen. What was the point of confronting Caitlin and telling her she knew there'd been something else in her hand? Caitlin would just come up with another story.

At the ring of the oven timer, Margaret took the pizza out and cut it into slices. She had to realize that Caitlin was only seven, insecure and upset with Sandy's being away.

She decided she wouldn't say anything about the mysterious piece of paper. Not right now, anyway.

Margaret ignored the small voice echoing at the back of her mind that suggested Caitlin wasn't an ordinary seven-year-old. Somehow she knew she would live to regret it.

JAKE DROVE down the mountain toward town. Rain was still falling heavily enough to keep the windshield wipers busy and make the narrow road surface dangerously slick. He had to pay close attention to his driving. Not much traffic along the road, not even on the highway.

He was thinking about Margaret—her unconventional beauty. Her hair was that rare true black with a sheen like silk. Its heavy masses framed her smooth face, modeled with precise delicacy. And those eyes...huge smoky and green, black lashed. Tiger eyes. Robert must have been crazy to give her up.

He wasn't aware that he was smiling faintly as he drove past the town green. The church fair was over; the booths and games removed. Every bit of refuse had been picked up, and the grass glowed greenly in the rain-drenched night air. Only the sign remained, flapping wetly in drizzle between two huge maple trees.

In the back of his mind he heard Margaret's voice describing the fortune-teller, Madame Zorina.

On an impulse he pulled the car over by the curb and turned off the engine. There was a second-hand bookstore half a block back. He got out and dashed toward the dimly lit storefront. The bell tinkled as he closed the door behind him, nodding to the woman behind the counter. "Good evening." She smiled and immersed herself once more in her paperback. Clearly a late customer couldn't compare with the exploits of her detective-hero.

Jake was a compulsive book buyer. Back in his apartment in New Haven, he had stacks of books, so many they wouldn't all fit in the shelves. He kept meaning to arrange his books in some kind of order.

He walked down the narrow aisles in the bookstore, knowing he could waste the rest of the evening here. He plucked a copy of *Bleak House* from the shelf and a paperback of Agee's *A Death in the Family,* before he found the Occult shelf. Assorted volumes, including a large, blue *History of Witchcraft,* and another on palmistry and Tarot. Not that he seriously believed Madame Zorina was a real witch, but she'd known Margaret's name. Of course, someone in town could have mentioned that she was taking care of Caitlin.

Carrying the four books, he walked back to the cash register. His footsteps echoed on the dusty floor. Outside, rain was pounding on the windowpane, shining like diamonds. The clerk looked up as he approached. "Find something you like?"

"Just these four." He placed the books on the counter. "You probably don't get many people buying books on witchcraft and palm reading."

Shifting the pile of books, she glanced at their spines. "Not many, but you'd be surprised what interests people."

"I noticed a fortune-telling booth at the fair today," he said pleasantly.

"Oh, Madame Zorina?" The clerk gave him an obscure smile. "What did you think of her? Oh, that's an even five dollars."

"Very impressive, I admit." He got out his wallet.

"Ugly as hell and a real crackpot, but if she told your fortune—" The clerk shrugged. "I'd pay attention if she said not to fly anywhere. Not that I believe everything she says, but there's *something* about her predictions. People laugh, and maybe she does mix in a few whoppers just to make things sound spectacular. But every once in a while she sees things. She read my palm and everything she saw was right on target. She said the man I was seeing wasn't trustworthy, that he really disliked women. I found out Madame Zorina was right. And she told me I would come into money. Not two weeks later my uncle died and left me this place. I've been selling books here ever since."

"It could be a form of mental telepathy."

The clerk shrugged. "Emotional atmosphere, something you can't explain in ordinary terms. Just because you can't see something doesn't mean it's not there. The air we breathe." She rang up the sale and closed the cash register drawer. "Maybe Madame Zorina tunes in on things that are invisible to the rest of us."

He picked up the stack of books and turned to go. "Is she ever wrong about her predictions?"

"Sure." The clerk chuckled. "Last summer she pestered the fire department for weeks. Said she'd had a vision that the town would be hit by a flood. No one paid her any mind, then the volunteer firemen were hit by a flood—one of their hoses sprang about a thousand leaks, flooding out Harvey's barn over in South Hollow."

Jake frowned and shifted the books under his arm. "She sounds like she's off her rocker."

"Who knows. Maybe she is." The clerk picked up her paperback. "But like I said, if she told me not to take any plane rides for a while, I wouldn't get on one for a million bucks."

MARGARET AND CAITLIN ate their pizza in front of the TV. It was eight o'clock when *Escape to Witch Mountain* ended, and Caitlin declared she wasn't a bit sleepy, so Margaret let her stay up and watch another movie.

Sorting through the shelf of video tapes, Margaret found *Dial M for Murder.* She put it in and pushed the Play button. "It's twenty years old and black and white, but it's a classic."

Caitlin rolled her eyes. "It's dumb. I saw it ages ago, and I didn't even like it."

"Too bad." Margaret sat down on the sofa. "Maybe you'd rather go write in your notebook or play with Barbie."

"Maybe I will." Caitlin yawned, suiting her actions to her words and heading toward the stairs. "Good night."

Margaret frowned. There'd been something fake about that wide yawn. She certainly was up to something. Unfortunately with Caitlin the possibilities for mischief were endless. She'd better go up and check on her in a little while just to make sure she hadn't climbed out the window and taken off for the quarry again and another forbidden boat ride. After a moment she called up after Caitlin, "I'll be up to tuck you in bed in a few minutes."

"Okay." Caitlin's voice floated downstairs, then her bedroom door slammed, and Margaret sat and watched the TV with a blank stare. Her mind wandered, and she thought of Sandy and Robert. Most likely they would call tonight, and then she would tell them about Jake McCall's visit. How would Robert react to the news? she wondered. The sudden appearance of an ex-brother-in-law he'd never mentioned. He'd probably told Sandy about his first wife by this time, that she'd died during an asthma attack.

But what if he hadn't?

She got up and pushed the Power button on the VCR, then turned the TV off. Funny, she had a strange, almost superstitious reluctance to tell Sandy and Robert about Jake.

Sandy had gone through so much with her nagging illness. She'd looked so pale and thin, and poor Robert was clearly worried about her health.

Margaret still couldn't make up her mind. Picking up the supper dishes she took them out to the kitchen and mopped up dried grape jam on the floor in front of the refrigerator where Caitlin had dropped it. All the while the thought of Jake McCall hovered in the back of her mind. His strong, lean face alert and compassionate. She sighed as she put the mop away.

She went upstairs to check on Caitlin. Her bedroom door was closed, and when she opened it quietly, her niece was curled under the covers, deep in sleep. Margaret dropped a kiss on her freckled nose and crept out into the hall again, leaving the door slightly open. Caitlin might wake in the night and call out.

She went downstairs and turned off the lights and locked the house up for the night. Then she curled up on the bed with a paperback mystery until after midnight, waiting for a call from Sandy. But the phone never rang. Finally she fell into exhausted sleep, and maybe it was the storm—the wind had strengthened, rattling dead branches off the big sugar maples in the driveway—but when she fell asleep, she began to dream a terrible nightmare.

She'd come home from work and entered her apartment in Boston, walking into the living room. Only somehow, it was Mrs. Knox's living room, with the crewelwork draperies, the piano, the ticking clock. And she was overcome by the most deadly fear she'd ever known. Sandy was sitting on the Hepplewhite settee, only it wasn't her sister at all. It was a big, stuffed doll that looked like Grace Kelly.

The French door was open, the draperies billowing. Someone had just left. She ran through the house calling frantically for Sandy. But each room she went into was empty.

She woke with a start, covered with clammy perspiration, shuddering... and heard Caitlin crying, "Mommy..." Margaret got out of bed and pulled her robe on, then ran down to Caitlin's room. Her niece was sitting up in bed, rubbing her eyes, still sobbing her heart out. "I... I had a bad dream," she gulped as Margaret took her in her arms.

"It's okay, I'm here now. The bad dream's all gone." She rocked Caitlin back and forth, kissing her cheek. "See? Everything's fine now."

Caitlin glared up at her. "How can everything be okay when Mom's still married to Robert? I *hate* him! He's awful, he hogs all the dessert, even when there's enough for me to have seconds. How would you like it if he was your stepfather and pinched you when no one was looking? He's a mean old pig, and I hate him, I'll always hate him! I don't care what Mom says or you say, he *stinks!*" The rest of her mumbled complaints trailed off in a hiccuping wail.

"Shush, it's okay, I've got you. Nothing's as bad as that, honey." Margaret hugged Caitlin, brushing back her rumpled hair with her lips. "It's probably pizza that gave you bad dreams. You ate too much."

Caitlin shook her head and sniffed. "I like pizza. It's Robert. That's why I have bad dreams, because he's my stepfather and I hate his guts."

Margaret settled herself more comfortably on the bed, nudging something bulky under the blanket with her knee as she pulled Margaret back against her breast and rocked her. "It was the storm, that's all. But the rain sounds lovely on the roof. Hear it pattering? It's like a lullaby. Hush now, darling. Try and go back to sleep."

She kissed Caitlin's forehead and laid her back down among the covers again. She didn't dare get into an argument about Robert again. It was none of her business, anyway, whether Caitlin accepted him as her stepfather or not. That was Sandy's problem, thank God.

Caitlin sniffled once or twice, then fell back to sleep, curled up among the blankets like a cherub. Which only proved appearances were deceptive, Margaret thought tiredly as she crawled carefully off the bed, trying not to wake her again. But her foot caught the edge of the bulky object under the bedspread and knocked it onto the floor.

It was a shoebox, and its contents spilled out onto the rag rug. She glanced up at Caitlin, but her niece's even breathing never faltered. She was dead to the world.

Margaret got down on her knees to gather up everything and put it all back without waking her. All sorts of odds and ends dear to a seven-year-old's heart, she thought wryly. A matchbook, an empty cigarette pack, Ninja Turtle cards, and an outdated itinerary from... She peered at the thin sheet of paper in the dim light from the hallway. A Rutland travel agency—Gateway Tours—for a trip to St. Kitts and Martinique, dated two years ago. A folded letter, probably the white paper Caitlin had been hiding behind her back earlier, and a black and white snapshot of...Robert. He had a mustache in the picture and was standing in front of Mrs. Knox's house! Robert said he'd never seen this house before the real estate agent showed it to them.

She tilted the picture toward the light and looked at it again. The upper left corner was torn, and it was crumpled. Clearly Caitlin had done her best to straighten the creases. Robert was looking slightly away from the camera as if he hadn't known his picture was being taken. The focus was blurred, but the house in the background was definitely Mrs. Knox's and the man was Robert with a mustache.

She tumbled everything back in the shoebox and tucked it carefully under the bedspread by Caitlin's feet. Now was not the time to tackle Caitlin about this. Obviously this was the booty she'd gathered through her ceaseless snooping. If she wanted to find out everything she could about the landlady, nothing would stop her.

Margaret went into the hall and noticed a slight draft from downstairs. A loose shutter began banging against the house, then a dead tree limb thudded onto the roof. She went downstairs, yawning widely. Her mind couldn't stop thinking about the photograph. It must have been taken a while ago. He'd never had a mustache in all the time she'd known him. And why had he pretended he'd never been in this house before they'd rented it? She remembered how he'd been unable to even recall Mrs. Knox's name. He'd turned to Sandy. "You know, darling, Mrs.... the owner of the house...."

She reached the bottom step and decided not to think about it anymore. There was a definite draft coming from down the hall. The air was colder, and there was an eerie sensation engulfing her.

Margaret switched on the overhead chandelier. It swayed slightly, crystal droplets tinkling in the stream of wind.

She followed the trail of cold air into the living room and saw that the French door had blown wide open. She closed it tightly and went into the kitchen. The window over the sink yawned wide; cold air blew in and out, knocking over several pots of herbs. Dirt littered the counter and floor.

"Oh, no! What a mess!" She leaned over the sink and closed the window before sweeping up the dirt and remains of the herbs. Then she noticed the cellar door was open, too. Somehow that was the last straw.

Margaret stood at the top of the stairs, shivering in her quilted robe, in a state of near panic. Below, the cellar lay in nightmarish darkness. She tried the light switch on the wall, but the bulb had burned out, and it was set so high in the ceiling it would take a human fly to reach it.

There was a flashlight in the counter drawer, but the batteries were almost dead. She shook it, and the beam brightened; but after only a few seconds it flickered and settled into a dim yellowish glow. Margaret glanced at the kitchen clock. Three a.m. That settled it. No way was she going down those stairs, no matter how many windows were open down there. She heard a slight clinking noise from somewhere in that yawning darkness. A fallen branch hitting a cellar window? Wild horses couldn't drag her down those stairs.

She shut the door tightly, blocking out a mental picture of thieves breaking into the cellar.

Suddenly the shutter stopped banging. All was quiet. She sighed and went back upstairs. Thank God Caitlin had slept through the whole thing. She peeked in the half-open door of her room. Yes, there she was, still sleeping like a baby. She prayed Caitlin would stay that way for the rest of the night and went down the hall to her room.

DOWNSTAIRS IN THE CELLAR the woman who'd tripped over the carton of old whiskey bottles rubbed her ankle, swearing softly. That had been too damned close. If that interfering idiot had come down and found her prowling around, she'd have had a hell of a time explaining what she was doing.

In the dark her eyes were angry, then calculating. She removed a tiny pencil flashlight from her coat pocket and slowly scanned the dimly lit cellar as the gas-fired old furnace kicked on suddenly with a roar.

There was a small door next to the furnace, but the woman ignored it, knowing it led to an old fruit cellar. She started edging up the stairs. It was unlikely the door had been left unlocked, but worth a try. She turned the knob, but it didn't budge. Either she got the door open, or she would have to try some other means of getting into the main house.

Luckily the door was old and ill fitting in its frame. Her plastic credit card worked nicely and edged the bolt back with only a muted click. She pushed the door open and found her way to the kitchen. The table and chairs were barely discernible in the dark. She continued down the hallway, gauging the distance in the blackness. Using the flashlight sparingly, she took great care not to allow the beam anywhere near the windows. The house was quiet, and everyone should be in bed. She looked at the luminous dial of her wristwatch—three-thirty. Which gave her plenty of time to search downstairs.

A subtle gradation of grays and blacks indicated the white-painted risers of the front staircase. She worked her way through the living room, dining room, then the den. She ran the flashlight along the bookshelves on the far wall. Dozens of paperbacks, some hardcovers. Books on gardening, art, travel, all aligned carefully—except for one volume that protruded from the shelf, by maybe half an inch. A big, red dictionary.

Picking up the book by its spine, she tucked it under her arm and searched carefully in the space where the book had been. Her fingers found nothing, and she began pulling other books out, throwing them to the floor without thought. Soon the shelf was bare.

She ran the flashlight's beam over its surface, cursing softly, "Where the hell is it?" She seemed to sway with a mixture of sheer rage and fear, then took a deep breath to collect her wits. Composing herself, she took a quick look toward the hall to make sure she hadn't wakened anyone when she'd tossed the books on the floor. All was as quiet as a tomb. She gathered up the books and stuck them back on the shelf, but not in the same order. There wasn't time for that. She would take one more encompassing look before she was done. She stretched out a manicured hand and straightened the dictionary, wondering if *he'd* found them, the damn bastard.

Well, there were other, more pressing things to be taken care of, including a cold-blooded murder; but it wouldn't be her first killing—and she suspected it wouldn't be her last.

She walked silently across the worn oriental rug to the front hall, catching a glimpse of her ghostly reflection in the gold-framed mirror on the wall, and laughed softly. Then she opened the door and let herself out of the house.

Chapter Five

In the morning Margaret stood staring at the front doorknob. She felt a jag of fear like a knife in the stomach. The door was unlocked, but she remembered locking it before she went up to bed last night. Someone had been in the house while she and Caitlin had been asleep!

She swallowed hard, studying the hallway. Everything looked normal. But someone had to have been in the house last night.

Really frightened now, she went through the house, room by room, looking for anything missing or out of place. Nothing seemed to have been touched or stolen. Mrs. Knox's silverware still rested in the dining room sideboard. The TV, stereo and VCR were still in the den.

"What are you doing?" Caitlin asked from behind her.

Margaret almost jumped out of her skin. She took a deep breath and turned around. "I put a book down somewhere and can't remember where I left it." Carefully conversational, she went on, "That storm last night was awful, wasn't it? The kitchen window blew open and knocked the plants all over the floor. Honey, you didn't unlock the front door when you came downstairs, did you?'' Caitlin was wearing her heart-shaped sunglasses. They waggled from side to side when she said no. "Oh, then I must have done it myself." Margaret gave a smiling shrug. "What do you want for breakfast—cereal or pancakes?"

A HALF HOUR LATER Margaret was washing the breakfast dishes and getting up the courage to go down the cellar stairs to check for broken windows when the phone rang.

A woman's voice said expectantly, "Polly?"

"I'm sorry, Mrs. Knox isn't here."

"Oh...well, uh, to whom am I speaking?"

"Margaret Webster. Who is this, please?"

"Where is Mrs. Knox, and when will she be back?" the woman said rudely.

"I don't give out information to strangers," Margaret replied, her voice crisp.

There was a small pause before the caller said, "Well, then I might—thank you very much." The receiver went down with a bang.

Margaret frowned and hung up. What was that all about? She really couldn't think about the caller. There was a more immediate problem on her hands. Should she call the police about the door? And tell them what, exactly. That she'd found it unlocked? They would thank her politely for reporting it and decide she was a nut, the type of hysterical woman who looked under her bed every night.

She put the last dish away just as a horrendous crash erupted from the other side of the house. Caitlin was at it again!

She ran down the hall and caught her niece standing on the edge of a chair, reaching up into the hall closet for something. The chair was teetering back and forth as Margaret dashed up to catch Caitlin before she fell. But the chair skidded and they both tumbled to the floor, landing on several boxes of games and puzzles that had already fallen off the closet shelf. There was an odd creaking sound, and Margaret glanced up in time to see the rest of the shelf come down, as well.

She grabbed Caitlin, shielding her quickly as a glass punch bowl whizzed past, a framed photograph, woolly hats, and lastly, what looked like a partial afghan, with the crochet hook still stuck in it.

Luckily Caitlin was unhurt. The punch bowl and photograph hadn't been so lucky. They lay on the floor, smashed to pieces. Margaret counted to ten and helped her niece up. "Get me a broom, pronto."

"I was only—"

"Never mind what you were doing. I'm trying hard not to spank you, Caitlin. Now go get a broom and dustpan."

Margaret swept up the glass and tried to control her temper while Caitlin stood by, explaining how it hadn't actually been her fault. "I was shooting a paper airplane, and it went up in the closet. So I had to get the chair and climb on it to reach high enough to get it down off the shelf. I didn't want to bother you because I knew you'd get mad."

Margaret leaned on the broom and fixed Caitlin with a fiery green stare. "The whole mess could have been avoided if you'd asked for help." She looked around at the dismal pile of broken glass on the floor—and there was no sign of a paper airplane anywhere. She strongly suspected it had never existed in the first place. "Where's the plane?" she asked accusingly.

Caitlin craned her neck and peered up where the shelf had been, as if she expected to see the fictitious plane still circling, like a tiny jet over a fogbound airport. "Wow, it's gone! Maybe it didn't go into the closet at all. Maybe it flew into the living room, instead."

Margaret gritted her teeth and put the shelf and its contents back up in the closet, then she dumped the shattered remains of the punch bowl and picture glass into the garbage. She went back into the living room to find Caitlin innocently writing in her notebook. "I think it's time we had a talk." But even as she opened her mouth to deliver a stern lecture on privacy and the responsibility of living in someone else's house, she knew it was a mistake. If she admitted to looking through the contents of the shoebox, Caitlin would go underground like a mole and Margaret would have no idea what she was up to. If she hammered away about Mrs. Knox, and how Caitlin shouldn't be snooping into the woman's belongings, inevitably she would say the wrong thing and Caitlin would redouble her efforts to find out all she could about the poor woman.

But it was too late now; she'd already started the lecture. So she droned on, emphasizing the need for honesty. When she ran out of breath and ideas, Caitlin asked, "Do you want to play gin rummy?"

Margaret stared at her, exasperated, feeling at her wits' end. What in the world was she going to do about Caitlin? She was tired of being bamboozled and bullied by a seven-year-old, and blurted out, "What exactly is in that notebook of yours. Don't bother telling me it's a secret. I don't want to hear any more of that nonsense."

Caitlin eyed her warily. "Uh, I told you. I'm gonna be a writer when I grow up, and I've decided I'm gonna write mysteries. So I'm collecting clues and stuff."

"About what mystery in particular?"

Caitlin took a dim view of this line of questioning. Frowning, she pushed the heart-shaped sunglasses back up on her nose, fiddled with the notebook cover and kicked at the leg of the Hepplewhite settee. Finally she said grudgingly, "Okay, I might as well tell you. You're gonna find out, anyway. It's about Mrs. Knox."

"What about Mrs. Knox," Margaret said with dawning horror.

"Well, she's *dead*, of course. Robert killed her. Here, see for yourself." She shoved the open notebook into Margaret's lap.

Margaret stared at the notebook in disbelief. It seemed to be partly in some rudimentary code, appealing no doubt to Caitlin's sense of the dramatic, and all about the probable whereabouts of Mrs. Knox.

Caitlin had written at the top of the page "Caitlin Ashley Emerson" in as fancy a script as she could. Underneath she'd printed a painstaking list:

P. Knox, t.y. ago, w. P.M.!
Psnd? Stbd? Kdnpd?
In Qry???
In lynbyn?
Buryd alve???

Margaret shut the notebook with a decisive snap. "This is ridiculous. The woman's in Europe."

Caitlin smiled. "Ha! That's what Robert wants everyone to think."

"What's your stepfather got to do with this?"

"Everything! He killed her, see?" Caitlin opened the notebook again to the appropriate page and tapped the first item on the list. "Two years ago Mrs. Knox *wasn't* Mrs. Knox. She was Polly Merrill. I know because..." She paused and shot Margaret another wary look. "Never mind how I found out. I know, that's all. Her name *was* Polly Merrill. Then she met Wendell Knox. He was rich and he owned this house with his wife, Martha. They were both old, but Martha was real sick. That's their picture that got broke in the closet just now."

"Oh, really," Margaret commented dryly.

"Yeah, well, Polly Merrill was a nurse. Remember, I told you about the uniforms I saw in her closet?" Margaret nodded dumbly, and Caitlin prattled on. "Polly got to be Martha's nurse, and then Martha died. Remember my friend Nancy?" Margaret found herself nodding again. "Well, Nancy said her mom said Polly knew a good thing when she saw it and latched on to Wendell before he knew what hit him. He married her, then he died, too. And that's how Polly got to be rich."

"That still doesn't explain why Robert would want to kill the woman. He doesn't even know her." Margaret shook her head in disgust.

Caitlin chewed on her lip in silence for a moment, then said with an air reminiscent of Sherlock Holmes cluing in the bumbling Dr. Watson to the obvious particulars of their current case, "I happen to have other stuff, proof he knows Polly. Only it's *knew* now, on account of she's prob'ly dead. Even if he didn't stab her or shoot her or anything, he prob'ly locked her up in a dark dungeon full of rats, where she starved to death, or he buried her alive, or something. Maybe he killed her and dumped the body in the quarry after he got her to go for a boat ride. That's why the boat's still there. He didn't feel like putting it away." Caitlin's eyes gleamed behind her sunglasses. "That's proof she's dead. Mrs. Knox would have put the boat away like you're s'posed to, right?"

Margaret took a deep, bottom-of-the-lungs breath. She glanced from Caitlin's stubborn expression to the notebook in her lap and then to the shoebox—that no doubt contained the proof Caitlin was talking about.

Margaret opened her mouth, but nothing came out. She just sat there, shocked and stunned. Caitlin's obsession with Mrs. Knox had obviously gone too far. If only she could talk to Sandy and get help dealing with all this! She cleared her throat, racking her mind for something intelligent to say. "Uh...look, your theory about Polly Knox—none of it would explain Robert's wanting to kill her."

"He's *mean and rotten,* that's why! They prob'ly fought...well, I know for a fact they had fights about money. Never mind how I know, I just do. Robert prob'ly wanted all Polly's money, and she wanted to spend some on her trip to Europe." Caitlin yawned, then said affably, "So he killed her dead."

Margaret stared at her in disbelief. "Because he didn't want her to spend her money on a trip to Europe? Come on, Caitlin! You just don't like Robert. Mrs. Knox would have to leave a will making Robert her heir, before he'd inherit anything." She shook her head. "Not one word of this makes sense. Why am I sitting here arguing about this. I must be crazy."

Snatching back her notebook, Caitlin jumped to her feet in sudden anger. "Okay, don't believe me! I don't care! Robert will get away with the perfect murder, and it'll be all your fault! And he might even hurt Mom to get her money, too. He tells lies all the time! When Mom was so sick he didn't even call the doctor—even though he told her he did." She gulped for breath and rushed on furiously. "It was all a big fat lie! I hid on the stairs and watched him pretend to dial. *He lied, lied, lied all the time, and I hate him!*" Caitlin turned and ran down the hall and upstairs. Seconds later her bedroom door slammed.

Margaret fought the urge to rush after her and talk this out once and for all. But Caitlin was too upset and angry; she would never listen to reason. Her imagination had conjured up this mountain of preposterous accusations and lies about Robert.

Sandy had warned Margaret that Caitlin went overboard at times with her pretending. Taking a deep breath, Margaret wondered if her niece had gone to Sandy with the same ridiculous stories about Robert. And if she had, why hadn't Sandy told her?

Caitlin, Sandy and Robert really needed to talk out their problems. Either that, or Caitlin would drive them all crazy.

DOWN BY THE RIVER in the white Victorian house, Madame Zorina passed her ringed hands over a crystal ball. She was breathing heavily, eyes focused on the swirling clouds within. "Come on, I ain't got all day. Whaddaya see?" Vern Boyce stared across the table, eyes narrowed in resentment.

"I see many things." Madame Zorina breathed deeply. "Children's games, nursery rhymes...'A B C, tumble-down D...'" When she spoke, her breath stirred the black lace draped over her orange hair and made it tremble. "*D* stands for *death,* Vern. That's what I see. It's here in the crystal. *You, terrible danger, death!*"

He flinched, the cords standing out in his neck. "Yer lyin'. There ain't nothin' in that crystal ball. I told ya before, there's big money comin' my way. I ain't doin' nothin' to spoil things." His smirk revealed grimy teeth. "I ain't got time for your nonsense."

"Death will come." Her voice shook with emotion.

Sweat broke out on Vern's brow. He brought his fist down on the table hard, making the crystal ball shake. "Listen to me, old lady. I know something and it means big money."

"No." She shook her head and folded her hands in her lap. "It means *death.*"

MARGARET WAS still sitting on the Hepplewhite settee when the hall clock struck noon. She felt unsettled and worried—especially about the unlocked front door. She knew she'd better make lunch before she scared herself to death.

About half an hour later Caitlin came downstairs just as Margaret took open-faced bacon, tomato and cheese sandwiches out of the oven. Sending Margaret a grumpy look, she said, "I don't want to talk about my notebook and Robert anymore. I'm hungry. I want—"

With a smile Margaret went over and gave her a big hug. "Lunch. Okay, I'll feed you, and I promise not to say one word about your notebook. Sit down while I get the milk." She slid the sandwiches on two plates and looked around. Caitlin was standing on the stool by the counter, examining the wall calendar.

"When's the next full moon?" she asked curiously.

Surprised, Margaret walked over and took a look. Finding the tiny full moon, she tapped the calendar. "Here, next Monday. Why?"

Caitlin got down, in the process knocking over the nearby flour and sugar tins. White powder cascaded everywhere, and by the time Margaret got it all cleaned up, Caitlin was halfway through her sandwich. She shot a quick look at her aunt. "Want to know why I asked 'bout the full moon?"

Margaret sat down across the table, the pleasant aroma of toasted tomato and cheese curling up between them. She was afraid to ask.

"Of course, if you don't want to know . . ." Caitlin mumbled past a mouthful of sandwich.

"Okay," Margaret conceded with a tired sigh. "What's the big deal about the next full moon?"

Caitlin leaned forward, eyes gleaming with excitement. "Madame Zorina, natur'ly. She said it means *danger*, remember? She even knew your name, so she prob'ly knows all kinds of stuff. She said I was a . . . a cantaloupe or something. What did she say I was?"

Margaret groaned mentally, then swallowed hard and said, "A catalyst."

"What's that?" Caitlin demanded.

"An expert at driving me crazy. No, it means you make things happen. At least she got that part right." Margaret managed to catch Caitlin's glass of milk just as she was about to knock it over.

"I've got a neat idea." Caitlin eyed the wall phone. "Why don't we call her up and ask her to tell the rest of my fortune. She prob'ly got over being tired by now."

"I don't think that's such a great idea," Margaret said thinly.

Just then the phone rang, and Caitlin grabbed it, shouting into the receiver rudely, *"Who's this?"* She listened for a second, then handed it to Margaret. "It's for you. Some dumb man."

The dumb man was Jake McCall. She could hear the smile in his deep voice. "Hi, I thought you might like to go out to dinner. That's of course, if you can get someone to stay with Caitlin."

Margaret hesitated. Somehow his voice sounded different over the phone, deeper, more intimate. She found that her hand holding the receiver was trembling slightly. Before she gave in to any second thoughts she said firmly, "Yes, I think I can get someone.'' It would be a relief to get out of the house, even for an hour or so, and Mrs. Till could probably come in for the evening. She'd said she was available most nights for baby-sitting.

Besides, it would be the perfect chance to talk to someone who could be objective about Caitlin's ridiculous obsession about Robert and Mrs. Knox. She turned and glanced over her shoulder at Caitlin who was busy pulling clothes off one of her Barbie dolls. That absorbed pose didn't fool Margaret. Her ears were flapping a mile a minute. She was dying to know what they were talking about.

''How about the inn down in Rochester?'' Jake murmured in her ear. ''They have really good seafood. I could pick you up about seven.''

''I'll have to call Mrs. Till, but if she's busy and can't stay with Caitlin, I could make dinner for us here,'' Margaret suggested. Her cooking was strictly utilitarian, nothing fancy.

He laughed. ''Let's hope your baby-sitter's available. Not to cast aspersions on your cooking, but I have a feeling Caitlin would be underfoot all evening.''

''Exactly.''

He laughed again, and Margaret felt a treacherous weakness in her knees. They talked for a few more moments, then Jake hung up and Margaret turned to see Caitlin watching her. With an effort she brought her mind back from its sidetrack of Jake's lean face, his piercing eyes and rich deep voice.

Caitlin shrugged her shoulders in disgust. ''Dumb love stuff!''

"I sincerely hope so," she agreed gravely, her green eyes laughing. Just then the front doorbell rang. She told Caitlin to stay in the kitchen while she answered it. A tall, stooped man stood on the porch. He had weather-beaten features and wore overalls and an old red and black lumber jacket. He nodded and took off his cap.

"The name's Vern Boyce. I'm Mrs. Knox's handyman. Thought I'd stop by after last night's storm and clean up the yard. Mrs. Knox likes me to keep the place tidy lookin'."

Margaret gave him a curious look. Sandy hadn't mentioned a handyman, and there was something unpleasantly sly about his dark eyes, as if he was secretly laughing at her. "I'm sorry, I don't know anything about a handyman." She went to close the door, and he pushed it open with a large, dirty hand. "What is it?" she asked steadily, every muscle of her body tense. She didn't like the way his narrowed gaze slid past her shoulder into the house. He swayed slightly, and from the strong odor of liquor on his breath, she realized he was very drunk.

"Mrs. Knox'll be real mad. She likes the place kept up nice." He grinned suddenly. "You stayin' here alone? Pretty lady like you? Gets lonely up here on the mountain. I could stop by, keep you company for a while if you like."

Caitlin had appeared in the hallway. That's all Margaret needed. Now she would have to explain drunken men to her. Margaret shoved the door shut quickly, missing the look of consternation on the man's angry face.

Caitlin frowned darkly. "Who was that?"

"Mrs. Knox's handyman." Margaret gave her a reassuring smile. "I said we didn't need him today."

"Oh." Caitlin stared at Margaret's white face for a long moment. "You were scared of him, weren't you?"

For a second Margaret considered denying it, then changed her mind. "Yes, I didn't like him or trust him. If he comes to the door again, don't let him in."

Caitlin nodded cautiously. It was on the tip of Margaret's tongue to ask if she knew if her mom had made arrangements with Mrs. Knox's handyman to keep the yard cleaned up, but Caitlin turned and went off to the kitchen without another word.

Shrugging her shoulders, Margaret watched from the window as Vern Boyce staggered out to his truck and drove off. She drew a sigh of relief and went downstairs to the cellar to look for broken windows while it was still daylight. Maybe she could fit some cardboard in place of any broken panes.

It was surprisingly dark at the foot of the stairs, even though it was barely two o'clock. A carton of empty whiskey bottles stood near one of the columns that held up the kitchen floor overhead. She shivered. It was cold down here, damp.

Several more cartons of bottles were stacked against the far wall. Why hadn't Mrs. Knox thrown them out? And how much did the woman drink?

She ducked under a cobweb and found a broken window. A branch was sticking through the hole in the glass. Carefully she removed the branch and tore a piece of cardboard from a carton. She fitted it over the broken pane. That would have to do for now.

Caitlin clattered down a few steps and looked around. "Wow, look at all the bottles. Do you think she drank all that before Robert killed her?"

Margaret frowned. "I thought we weren't going to talk about that nonsense anymore."

"Well, I forgot," Caitlin muttered offhandedly, wandering down another step or two. Margaret reached out a hand and grabbed her arm.

"No, you don't. This cellar is off-limits. Too many dark corners and glass bottles. Get back upstairs and don't poke that nose of yours down here again." They climbed back upstairs, Caitlin still arguing that dark corners never scared her, she was brave, she would be okay. Margaret didn't buy that argument and firmly locked the door behind them.

MARGARET WAS just fastening her earrings when the doorbell rang and Jake arrived, a little before seven-thirty that evening. With a critical eye she took one last look in the mirror. Her blue dress was an old favorite, falling in swingy folds to just below her knees. Maybe not the latest fashion, but it was comfortable, and she always felt good when she wore it.

She went downstairs and came face-to-face with Caitlin who was coming from the kitchen with a mug of hot chocolate. As she opened her mouth to warn her not to spill it, the contents sloshed over the rim. She closed her eyes, but when she opened them, Caitlin was still there. She prayed for patience. "Take that back to the kitchen and drink it. And bring a damp cloth to mop this up."

By this time Jake had appeared in the living room doorway. His gaze took in her appearance, the graceful line of her figure, the way her black hair shone in the light from the overhead chandelier. He smiled. "Hello."

"Hi, I'll be ready in a minute," she said apologetically. Pushing down a bewildering sense of familiarity and ease, she snatched up her coat and purse. The feeling was so strong her heart was pounding. "I'll be back around ten or so, Mrs. Till."

The housekeeper, whom Margaret had called and asked to baby-sit earlier that afternoon, was leading Caitlin off to the kitchen for a damp cloth as Jake held the front door open.

"Don't you worry, Miss Webster, we'll be just fine." Mrs. Till smiled comfortably and gave Caitlin a nudge down the hall. "Didn't I tell you to drink that in the kitchen? Land sakes, you never listen!"

THE RIDE TO TOWN was fairly short, as they'd decided to eat at the inn, a big, white-pillared establishment with a side terrace for summer dining.

Jake ushered her up the steps and inside. "Heard from Robert and Sandy yet?"

She shook her head no. "They're probably having too much fun, but I'm sure they'll call soon."

They ordered drinks and pea soup as a starter for grilled swordfish. At the small white-draped table Margaret slowly relaxed amid the murmur of conversation, soft laughter and the clink of cutlery.

It was a large room, half-full of diners. A huge fieldstone fireplace took up the middle of one wall. Flanking it were tall, black-glassed windows, which by daylight would reveal a spectacular view of mountain peaks and blue skies. Now the windows revealed a few bright stars and winking candlelight.

"How's your business going?" she asked pleasantly as their drinks arrived.

The waitress left and Jake said, "So-so. I'm involved with a project in downtown Rutland. They're talking massive reconstruction. It means tearing down quite a few buildings." Jake just stared and found himself looking directly into Margaret's eyes. They were extraordinary eyes, green as pools, fringed with thick black lashes.

"I thought you said you were a civil engineer. I didn't know they put up buildings."

He smiled. "Usually we're involved in things like roads, bridges, highways. Sometimes, though, we're called in if there's large-scale demolition."

"Dynamite and blowing up buildings? Sounds like a schoolboy's dream."

"Not quite, but pretty close," he admitted with another smile. "What do you do when you're not taking care of Caitlin?"

"Nothing as exciting as your job. I work for an insurance company in Boston." She gave a half laugh. "At least Caitlin's a change from insurance forms five days a week."

"Has she recovered from her boating adventure?"

She nodded. "I think so—" She looked up as the waitress placed the soup on the table. "As a matter of fact, I wanted to talk to you about something."

The waitress left and Jake glanced across the table at Margaret curiously.

"Caitlin doesn't like Robert. In fact, she seems to despise him." She gave a sad shrug. "I guess it's natural. She hardly sees her real father. And when Sandy married Robert, she probably thought she was losing her mother, too."

"They haven't been married long. Give her time, she'll come around."

"It's not just hurt feelings. Caitlin's making up stories, telling horrible lies about Robert."

"What sort of lies?" he asked, puzzled. She sighed and sat back in her chair. She wore a soft velvet dress of blue with bell-like sleeves and a deep neckline. Her skin was smooth and creamy. Her breasts moved softly beneath the heavy material as she shifted her shoulders. He said gently, "Come on, it's really bothering you. Tell me about it."

Reluctantly she met his gaze. "I'm just about at my wits' end with her. She's convinced Robert has killed the landlady, Mrs. Knox. She's collecting clues, writing her suspicions down in a notebook."

"Sounds serious. Robert might end up behind bars if he's not careful."

"It's not funny," she said, her green eyes wide and hurt.

"Okay," he said gravely. "But I wouldn't worry too much about her detective work. When the landlady returns, Caitlin will realize she was wrong. It's probably just a phase she's going through. Robert and your sister will have to deal with it."

She flicked him a noncommittal glance. Her body was tense, her fingers taut as she gripped her napkin, as if she felt she had to hang on to something. After a long moment she let out a breath. "Something else has me upset. I got up this morning and the front door was unlocked. I locked it last night before we went up to bed. Someone was in the house last night, I'm sure of it."

"Anything missing? Did you call the police?"

"Not that I could see. And I had no real proof, so I didn't call them." Her husky voice trailed off, her eyes brilliant in the candlelight.

"Caitlin might have left it open and forgot to tell you," he suggested quietly.

"I asked her, and she said she hadn't touched the door." She drew a deep breath, smiled ruefully and said, "God, I wish Sandy and Robert were home. I know my sister isn't well, but Robert could certainly handle things."

"Well, they'll be home soon. How'd you meet Robert, anyway?" he asked curiously.

She shrugged. "Downhill skiing, last year. I was at Killington with friends. Trail conditions were awful, wall-to-wall ice. I slid halfway down the mountain on my backside, then hit a tree and panicked. Everyone was back at the lodge. I was cold and scared, and Robert happened along, thank God. Calm and cheerful, he talked me down the rest of the way." She smiled in reminiscence. "I don't think I could have made it without him."

"He's a damn good skier. Rock-climbing, too," Jake said thoughtfully. "He's always been pretty much of a loner."

"He never had much family life. His father died or ran out on the family. His mother remarried when he was ten or so. He's been more or less on his own since he was a teenager." She smiled. "But he turned out all right, even without much of a stable home life."

"A terrific guy," Jake agreed, leaning back in his chair and stretching out his legs.

Margaret noted the smooth play of muscle and the long, lean lines of his body. Intimidating. She frowned and pushed the thought out of her mind. "Yes, charming, and a great sense of humor, too." She glanced at Jake and saw that his eyes were crinkled up in laughter.

"Are . . . you still in love with him?" His voice was quiet, his eyes no longer laughing.

She flushed. "No, I'm not. That's all over now." Her choice of the word *now* was instinctive and revealing. He didn't answer, and she flicked a quick look at him.

He was sipping his wine, gazing back at her almost abstractedly. She couldn't tell what he was thinking, and she picked up her fork and began to eat to cover her confusion. He was a virtual stranger, yet she felt as if she'd known him for years. She'd told him things she wouldn't have told anyone else.

Jake put his wineglass down. "I picked up new plugs for Robert's car. And a brake cable. Won't take me long to install, and I'll change the oil while I'm at it. Make sure the car's in good shape. You don't want to risk a breakdown while you're at the farm with Caitlin."

She nodded, and any constraints on their conversation seemed eased. They talked about Margaret's dream of owning an herb farm. "I love gardening," she admitted with a self-conscious half smile. "I know I'd be good at it."

"If your thumb's as green as your eyes, you're all set," he said quietly.

She spread her hands and smiled, then tilted her head. "What about you? Do you really want to build bridges and roads for the rest of your life?"

"It'll do for now. I have a cabin on the Maine seacoast where I go when the world closes in." His voice was low. "Do you like Maine?"

She nodded. "I haven't been there in years, though."

"We'll have to see what we can do about changing that," he said with a wide smile.

Jake paid the bill and they left the inn. The ride back to North Hollow and Quarry Farm seemed oddly short. Margaret felt so at ease with Jake, drawn to him, as if she'd known him all her life.

As he pulled the car into the driveway and switched off the engine, he turned his head and looked at her. "Stay a minute. There's just one thing..." He reached for her, cupping his hand around her soft cheek.

The thud of her heart sounded like thunder to her ears as her lips met his. Her lips parted, and all individual sensation—the warmth of his body against her breasts, the movements of his lips and tongue and hands, were swallowed up by an overwhelming wave of sheer physical pleasure.

When she went into the house a few minutes later, she could still feel the warm touch of his mouth on hers, like a luminous imprint no observer could miss. She could still feel it as she fell asleep hours later.

Chapter Six

Master detectives didn't need much sleep. They had to be awake practically at dawn, on the trail of evil master criminals. Caitlin's stomach rumbled, reminding her she'd only eaten three cookies, hardly enough to keep Sherlock Holmes going for long.

She'd got up really early. The kitchen clock said seven-thirty, and the sky was just turning a pearly gray outside the window over the sink. She took another cookie from the pantry and popped it in her mouth, chewing as she went back upstairs. Not back to her bedroom, of course. There were important clues to be searched for and found.

The attic, for instance, would be a good place to look. Mrs. Knox kept the attic door locked, but Caitlin had already taken the key, kept ordinarily in a drawer in the hall table. The key lay small and hard in her jeans pocket.

She mounted the stairs to the attic, picturing the master criminal—Robert—plotting in the attic with his evil gang. Master criminals always had a gang of evil cutthroats who sat around waiting for orders to wreak havoc on the innocent and unsuspecting.

Mrs. Knox had prob'ly been unsuspecting before Robert and his gang hit her in the head and heaved her in the quarry, she thought, swallowing the last morsel of cookie.

Sherlock Holmes or the Bloodhound Gang wouldn't be caught off guard like Mrs. Knox, no sir. She glanced around the upper hall, standing motionless for several seconds, ready for anything, even Robert's evil gang. Nothing stirred.

The attic door stood at the end of a short hallway, up two steps. The door was painted white and opened easily when Caitlin inserted the key. She stepped inside. The attic was a big room with an enormous brick chimney in the middle of the floor. Bulky cartons, trunks and rolled-up rugs were piled against one wall. Dusty furniture took up most of the space behind the chimney; and overhead, old clothing was hung from rods laid across exposed beams. Nothing much else to see but shadowy stacks of magazines and old newspapers.

Still, she had to steel herself for a few seconds before walking around the dusty attic. It was dark, hard for even a master detective to really see anything. She noticed a light switch on the wall and flipped it upward. Brilliance flooded down from an overhead light onto the jumble of cartons, old furniture and junk.

A wrought-iron garden chair stood near a tall cupboard with dusty glass doors. Glass objects glinted on the cupboard shelves. They looked like scientific stuff. Certainly, if Robert were a mad scientist trying to take over the world, which Caitlin dimly remembered from extensive comic book reading was their usual sinister aim, this stuff would be just what they'd use.

She looked around and spied an old trunk by the cupboard. Walking over to it, she tried the lock. Success! Opening the trunk, she was disappointed to only find yellowed magazines inside, dated May, 1945. She flipped through the pages, bored. There wasn't much to see. Advertisements for weird-looking cars and cigarettes.

She flipped a few more pages. The ladies in the pictures wore peculiar hairstyles and funny clothes. Dumping the magazines on the floor, she found clothes underneath. They smelled musty, like old perfume. There was a black dress with a lace collar, a fringed shawl. She reached way down, and her groping fingers touched something hard. A small wooden box with a curious design on the front.

The box was locked. The top wouldn't come off, no matter how hard Caitlin tugged. It was some kind of weird puzzle box.

But that wasn't a problem. She was good at puzzles. Master detectives had to be expert at that sort of stuff. You just had to figure out which square to push. Frowning harder, she sat down on the dusty floor and experimented further, pressing first one square of wood, then another.

Nothing happened. The lid wouldn't budge.

She thought a minute, then carefully pressed her fingers against every other square on the front of the box. Nothing. She sighed and thought harder, then tried pressing a different sequence of the squares. One after another—until she heard a tiny muted click and the lid popped up. She grinned and let out a breath she didn't realize she'd been holding.

There was a bunch of old papers in the box. She picked up the one on top, smoothing it out, her eyes getting bigger and bigger as she realized her name was written in bold ink on the worn paper.

JAKE HADN'T FORGOTTEN his promise to give the Fiat a tune-up and arrived just after eight a.m. He climbed the back steps and tapped on the door. "Margaret?"

She opened it, long black hair curling about her face. She wore a vivid blue shirt and jeans and looked delightful. "Hi."

"Thought I'd get started on the Fiat bright and early."

Her face took on a rosy flush and her green eyes smiled at him. "Wonderful, how about coffee?"

"Maybe later. I'd like to get started right away." He gestured toward the barn. "Does Robert keep any tools for the car there? Socket wrenches, screwdrivers?"

"I think so. There's a shelf just to the right by the door. You can't miss it. Right next to a set of old tires."

"I'll find it, no problem." With a wave he turned and crossed the yard to the big red barn. The door creaked as he slid it open. Dust motes swirled up and got in his eyes. Coughing slightly, he brushed a cobweb off his face and looked around. The shelf Margaret had mentioned was just to his right. A toolbox sat on the shelf. He opened it and got lucky when he found socket wrenches to fit the Fiat. The old tires leaning against the wall were probably Robert's, too.

He brushed dust off the sidewalls. The tires were in pretty good condition.

Ten minutes later he had the oil changed and had popped in a new air filter. A new cable for the safety brake lay in a box on the Fiat's front seat. He would install that after he checked the plugs and wires.

"I thought you could use some coffee." Margaret's voice brought him out of the depths of the engine. She smiled and handed him a mug. "How's everything going?"

He sighed. "Okay, I got the oil changed. It was practically sludge. Robert has run the car into the ground. He shouldn't have left this car for you to use."

She brushed a gentle finger across his cheek. "Every time I think about it, I want to scream. Lucky for me you came around." She touched his hair ever so gently. "I've got waffles cooking for Caitlin's breakfast. Got to get back to the kitchen. See you later."

Jake tried to concentrate on replacing the plugs and wires after Margaret left. But thoughts of her haunted him while he worked. He finally kept his mind on the job long enough to complete it, then turned his attention to the brake cable. While he was sliding the jack under the front axle, he noticed the cut on the side-wall of the left front tire.

He touched the cut. It was almost down to the fabric. The tire was fairly new and should still be under warranty. He opened the glove compartment. Robert might have left the sales slip and warranty there. Maybe Jake could get a new tire.

The compartment was a clutter of maps, rubber bands and dusty papers. He sorted through them. No sales slip.

But he did find a wristwatch which he recognized as soon as his fingers touched it. *Betsy's*. He suddenly felt sick to his stomach.

Jake held on to the watch and closed his eyes, rubbing his fingers gently across the leather band. In his mind he could still see Betsy wearing it....

Stunned, he put the watch back in the compartment. He then sat back on the seat, letting in a deep breath. This trip was taking its toll on him. He had to get hold of himself—and thinking of Margaret would help.

Needing something to do with his hands, Jake reached for the maintenance book in the glove compartment, unconsciously skimming the pages. When he went to put the manual back, he noticed a folded piece of paper on his lap, which had to have fallen out of the book. Unfolding the paper, he laughed when he saw that it was a tire sales slip and warranty from a store in Rutland. Great! He would go back to the store and get the tire replaced.

He folded the sales slip and put it in his pocket. As he was finishing attaching the brake cable, a beat-up pickup truck rattled up the drive. A skinny, unshaven man in a red and black lumber jacket got out and went up the back steps to the house.

Jake wiped his hands on a rag and took a step toward the house as the man began yelling and rattling the doorknob.

"Lemme in! I want money, lots of it! If you and Mrs. Knox wanna keep me quiet, you're gonna pay big! Goddamn it, I want what's comin' to me. A hundred thousand!" The man's voice was thick and slurring, and Jake realized the man was drunk and dangerous.

Margaret opened the door a crack. "I don't know what you're talking about. Go away! If you don't, I'm calling the police!"

By this time Jake had walked over and grabbed the drunk by the arm. "Better get on your way. The lady means what she says."

Boyce stumbled backward, shaking off Jake's hand. "Damn it, I want what's mine! They can fool some people, but not me—I want money to keep my mouth shut."

Jake raised his voice. "Call the police, Margaret."

Boyce shook his fist in fury, then stumbled over to his truck and drove off as Jake ran up the back steps. Margaret was standing in the kitchen, already on the phone.

"No, I told you, he was drunk and yelling threats. Restraining order? Yes, I'd appreciate that." She hung up and held her hand against her forehead for a moment. "They're sending an officer to Boyce's house to have a word with him. I can swear out a restraining order if he comes back."

Caitlin came into the kitchen, something small and wriggly in her hand. "Look, a worm! I found a new pet. I'll keep it. Maybe it'll have babies."

Margaret took a deep breath. "Worms need damp earth. They have to stay outside." She firmly ushered Caitlin out the back door. "Put it under the lilac bush. And when you come in, go upstairs and wash your hands."

Caitlin gave a bored shrug and looked up at Jake who smiled at her. "What's a 'straining order?"

"A legal term," he said with a wink. "Better put your worm under that lilac bush." She ran down the steps and around the side of the house, and he turned to Margaret. "Boyce is probably the neighborhood screwball. Once the police talk to him, he'll leave you alone. You don't have to be nervous. If he makes any more trouble, I'll pay him a visit."

"I'm not nervous," she said firmly. "I'm concerned. We're isolated up here, and I'm not taking any chances."

"Well, he's gone, and the police'll take care of things." He glanced at his wristwatch and then kissed her. When they both came up for air, he said ruefully, "I'm running late. I've got to go to Rutland for a new tire. I'll call you when I get back. In the meantime, the car's tuned up, and you shouldn't have any more trouble."

Caitlin came back in, wormless, just as Jake left. After being told twice to wash her hands, she waved them under the dripping faucet and dried them on her shirt. Then she sat down at the kitchen table and said nonchalantly, "What if the bottles in the cellar are that mean old man's? What if he hides in the cellar and drinks?"

"They're not his." Margaret gave her a suspicious look. "And when did you go down into the cellar again? I told you not to."

Caitlin buttered a piece of toast with unnecessary care. "Last night, while you were out with Mr. McCall. I thought I heard a funny noise, like a raccoon was down there. So I went and looked, but there wasn't any raccoon, only a whole lot of bottles." She looked up at Margaret and said, "What if they're really his, and he comes back?"

For a horrifying second a vision of Vern Boyce creeping around the cellar flashed through Margaret's mind, and fright made her voice sharp and angry. "They're not his, and he won't bother us anymore. I called the police."

BUT LATE THAT NIGHT, after darkness had fallen, Vern Boyce returned. He banged on the door with a hard fist, yelling, "You don't scare me none, lady. I know what's comin' to me. Where's Mrs. Knox? I want money, and I want it now!" His rheumy eyes glared at Margaret, who was peering out the window. "Mine! I'm only after what's mine. I could make big trouble if I tol' all I knew. You know wha's goin' on, *fraud*." He reared back and glared at her. "Zorina says yer nothin' but trouble."

"Go away. Mrs. Knox isn't here, and I don't have any money for you."

Boyce peered blearily at her and spoke in a low, mean snarl. "Zorina says there's terrible black fog comin' to swallow me up. I don' believe it. She ain't always right. I want my money! Hand it over, or I'll come in and get it!"

"Go away! I'm warning you, I'm calling the police!" She swallowed hard. Boyce's face was rigid with fury. His fist went back as if to smash the windowpane.

Then, suddenly, as if in answer to a prayer, headlights appeared down the road and slowed at the end of the driveway. Boyce grinned with satisfaction and said, "Looks like I'm gonna get what I come for!" He wove unsteadily down the back steps and out toward the car. Then, bending at the window by the driver's side, he appeared to hold a brief conversation.

Margaret dashed to the phone and dialed the police with shaking fingers. Oh, God, she thought frantically, if he came back from that car he would break the window and nothing could stop him.

For a moment fear made her legs rubbery, and she had to lean against the wall. Answer, she thought. Behind her the clock chimed eleven-fifteen p.m.

Damn the police! Why didn't they answer? She glanced out the window to see if Boyce was still there. The driveway was empty—the car and Boyce were gone.

Then the telephone line went dead.

VERN BOYCE climbed into the front seat of the car and slammed the door. "Just so's we unnerstan' each other. I want half."

"I said I'd give you half, didn't I?" The driver smiled and started the car, edging it up the track behind the barn. The engine growled softly as the car bounced over the rutted field, the headlights casting a yellow glow in the velvet blackness of night.

"Words come cheap. I don' trust nobody, less'n I see the color of their money." Grinning, Boyce patted his hip.

The driver's gaze moved fractionally downward and to the right. Boyce meant business. He had a *knife*.

It was fixed to his belt in a sheath over his left hip, where he could free it simply by snapping open the single narrow leather strap. In one second the blade could be slipped from the holder and wrapped tightly in his fist. In two seconds it could be jammed deep, slicing soft flesh.

Leaving the headlights on, the driver switched off the engine, and they got out of the car. Boyce turned and said with an uneasy laugh, "Funny place to hide money, up by the quarry."

Smiling reassuringly, the driver walked around the front of the car and joined Boyce on the dirt path. "Better than a bank these days. Negotiable securities, easy to cash, anonymous." The driver shrugged and said, "Can't do better than that."

They were standing at the edge of the headlight's glow. The night was chilly and silent, with only a half moon above. Boyce scowled. "Yeah, but why bury it up here?"

The moon went behind a cloud, hiding the driver's expression. "It's safe. Nobody's around this time of year." Even as the driver spoke, Boyce took the knife out of the sheath and held it in front of him.

They walked up the path into the shadowy darkness, Boyce a few steps ahead of the driver, who leaned down and silently picked up a large, flat rock.

The quarry lay just ahead, black as a grave.

Boyce took two steps and started to turn around, saying in a guttural, gravelly voice, "Ain't we gonna need a shovel? Hey, quit wastin' my time. Where's the money?"

Frowning, with a tense, predatory look on his face, Vern never got his answer as the driver swung the rock overhead, smashing it downward, full force, on his skull. He fell facedown in the weeds, and his knife flew out of his hands, sparkling for a moment in the glimmer of moonlight.

The ground was wet and thick with weeds as the killer leaned down and deliberately smashed Boyce again in the back of the head. The rock made a sickening dull noise as it cracked his skull open.

The killer let out a breath of relief and put the rock down. Boyce was definitely dead.

The only movement was the wind whispering in the trees. It took just a few seconds to roll the body over the edge of the quarry. A moment later the sound of a splash echoed from far below. Then the killer threw the rock and knife after the body and walked back down the path to the car.

Vern Boyce's murder had taken less than five minutes.

MARGARET STOOD in the doorway to Caitlin's room the next morning, frowning. It was time for breakfast, but she wasn't in the bathroom or anywhere upstairs. Where was she?

Ordinarily Caitlin's antics filled her with a blend of frustration, worry, and—once in a while—half-acknowledged amusement. This morning she was not amused. If she knew Caitlin—and she did—she was somewhere in the house, poking her nose into things that were none of her business.

Fuming, Margaret went downstairs. Where was she? "Caitlin?" When she walked into the living room, the French doors to the terrace were standing slightly open.

Immediately she thought of the quarry. Pulling a sweater on as she ran through the field behind the barn, she crashed through tangled weeds and grasses, then up the slope to where the path ended at the steep quarry.

Margaret's mind filled with nightmarish images of Caitlin lying facedown in the water. Oh God, what if it was already too late? No, she told herself. Everything would be all right. She would find her safe and sound.

By the time she looked over the edge of the quarry, Margaret was half out of her mind with fear.

The quiet, black waters lay far below, mirroring the blue Vermont sky and wisps of cloud drifting across it. She could see something floating on the surface, not Caitlin, thank God, but a bundle of old clothes, dark and sodden. Blue denim, red- and black-checked—a lumber jacket.

As if she wasn't really there, Margaret watched as a head gently bobbed up and down in the water as if in slow motion. She became hypnotized by its rocking— and then as reality set in, she found herself wide-eyed and as white as a ghost when she realized what she was staring at. Vern Boyce's body.

Not knowing where she found the strength, Margaret scrambled down the side of the quarry, breathing hard, panting, grabbing handholds of saplings, working her way closer to the body.

She didn't know what she could do. He was *dead.* Her stomach churned, and she fought back a wave of nausea as she reached the flat rock by the water's edge.

He must have fallen from the quarry rim, hitting... No, she wouldn't think about that. He might still be alive. She had to concentrate on trying to save him.

She got down on her knees and tried to grab his leg. The body bobbed up and down just out of reach in the lapping water as if he were a creature in a nightmare, as if she would wake up and find none of this was real.

Over her own gasping, she heard the sounds of birds twittering in the clump of birches on the far bank. The buzz of dragonflies and mosquitoes. Even the sweet scent of lilacs on the morning air. Overhead the sky was still beautiful. The same wisps of cloud drifted through the blue; the sun, rising in the east, was a dazzling gold.

It was only the quarry that was different, full of death. Her heart beat furiously, and she started shaking, shivering with fear.

Margaret took a deep breath and tried to control her shaking. Stretching her hand out farther, she managed to grasp his pants leg and pull him toward the rock. God, he was a big man, heavy. She would never get his body out of the water.

Her spine seemed to curve in horror as she forced her hands to grab hold of the soaked jacket, struggling to haul him up on the rock. His head banged against her left knee leaving a smear of blood. She swallowed bile and looked away from the bloody head and the reddish wet streak on her jeans. The body seemed to be stuck, snagged on some underwater projection, a branch or a rock. She yanked harder, and suddenly it broke free and slid upward with a disgusting wet sound that rubbed her nerves raw. She tried not to hear the noise it made sliding across the rock, tried not to look at that dead face. The eyes were open, staring. Quarry water dripped from his mouth.

Oh God, she thought, *I'm going to faint.* But that meant falling into the quarry or onto the body. She really didn't know which would be worse.

She closed her eyes and pulled, eventually managing to get the upper half of his torso onto the rock. Then she huddled there beside the body, unable to move, shuddering.

He was slumped halfway out of the water, his neck bent at an unlikely angle, the head sagging in a position that seemed anatomically wrong. A horrible sticky, bloody place marked the back of the head. Margaret had never seen a dead body before.

In the back of her throat she made a wet choking sound, which quickly grew into retching noises. She was thoroughly sick, vomiting into the water of the quarry. Her throat burned as she sat back on her heels, dizzy, weak and shivering with violent spasms of revulsion. Suddenly, from nowhere, she began to cry, gasping tears of shock and horror, the culmination of all the accumulated stress of the past few days.

CAITLIN WAS in the kitchen when she got back to the house. "Where have you been all this time?" Margaret demanded, wiping tears from her face with the back of her hand. Fat tears still tracked down her cheeks and settled saltily in the corners of her mouth, then dribbled over her chin. She hugged herself, then pulled a tissue from the box by the wall phone, blew her nose and got control of herself. "I said, *where were you?*"

Round-eyed with curiosity, Caitlin stared at her. A guilty look crossed her small, freckled face. "Uh, playing checkers. I'm real good, and I like it when it's my turn all the time. Uh, what's wrong? How come you're crying?''

Obviously Caitlin had been up to her usual tricks, but Margaret didn't have time to go up and check for Mrs. Knox's broken belongings. "Nothing's wrong," she said flatly, thinking this was the understatement of the year. "Go into the dining room and eat your breakfast. I have to make a phone call."

She closed the kitchen door and dialed the police. The line was working again, thank God. She could hear the click of the connection, but inside her head she kept seeing the back of Vern Boyce's head. And she couldn't seem to stop shaking. She drew deep breaths and, with an effort, banished the vision.

After she hung up the phone, she felt better, knowing help was on the way. She looked out the window when the squad car arrived, then told Caitlin there'd been an accident down the road and to go up to her room until the police left. Reluctantly Caitlin climbed the stairs, and when she heard the door close, Margaret went to the back door and let the police in.

The policeman was in uniform, powerfully built, blond, blue-eyed, with the hard, no-nonsense voice of a cop. He had his right hand on the gun at his hip. His eyes were direct, assessing. "Police. You called us?"

She nodded. "Yes, I'm Margaret Webster."

"This your house?"

"Well, no. My sister's renting it for the summer from Mrs. Knox. My sister's away with her husband on a trip. I'm just staying here while they're gone, watching their daughter."

"You say you found a body?"

"Yes, Vern Boyce." She gestured toward the field behind the barn. "In the quarry—he's dead."

The officer nodded again. "I'll take a look." He stepped off the back step and walked away through the field.

She closed the door and leaned against it. Her legs were trembling, and she was still so cold. She willed herself to walk to the counter and pour a cup of coffee. She drank it slowly and managed not to spill any.

A few minutes later she saw the policeman come back from the direction of the quarry. He reached in the open window of the squad car and spoke into the radio. Then he straightened and walked toward the house.

She opened the door and let him in. "He's dead, isn't he?" It wasn't really a question. No one could survive a head wound like that.

He nodded and got out a small notebook. "You have any idea what he was doing up there?"

"No. He was Mrs. Knox's handyman. He came around the other day, and last night...again. He was drunk. Maybe he wandered up there in the dark and fell in. His head—" she cleared her throat "—was badly injured. He wasn't breathing when I found him."

"Why would he be wandering up there in the dark?"

She felt she was losing some important advantage that she couldn't identify. She shrugged. "I don't know. He came around looking for work after that big storm on Wednesday. I sent him away."

The policeman gazed impassively at her, waiting. He didn't say anything, and the seconds stretched out. There was a vaguely uncomfortable silence. "And?"

She shrugged again, helplessly. "Well, he was drunk. I called the police station and reported it. Then last night, when he came back, I tried to call again, but the line was out. He was yelling threats, shouting. Frankly, I had no idea what he wanted."

"And you say Mrs. Knox is...?"

"I'm sorry, I'm not explaining this very well. She's in Europe." She swallowed hard, feeling an overwhelming sense of guilt. Why hadn't she made more of an effort to reach the police last night? If she'd tried again, say fifteen minutes later, maybe the line would have been working. The police would have come by, and Vern Boyce wouldn't have fallen in the quarry.

The policeman nodded. He jotted down a few more words, and said, "His truck's parked down the road a hundred yards or so. Keys still in it. We'll check and see if he ran out of gas, but if not, well, he probably came up here with something definite in mind... maybe to use your phone. Did he say anything about running out of gas? Did he ask to use the phone?"

She took a deep breath. "No. He didn't say anything about running out of gas. I *told* you, he was drunk. Nothing he said made sense. He kept talking about money. I didn't have any money for him."

The officer tucked the notepad into his breast pocket and looked out the door. Two police cars were pulling up, and an ambulance. He turned to go. "You'll be available if we need you?" Another question that wasn't really a question, and she nodded stiffly. "If the coroner finds alcohol in his blood, it could well be an accident. Boyce had a pretty good reputation as a drinker."

As Margaret closed the door behind the policeman, Caitlin said from behind her, "I saw a movie once about vampires. Want to know where they chomp you?"

"No, and I thought you were supposed to stay upstairs," Margaret said, briskly walking down the hall. She would do the laundry, vacuum, work her way through the day, and maybe she would forget what was burned into her memory.

"You said I could come down when the policeman left. Right on the neck, that's where they get you. Is that what happened to the man in the quarry?" Her eyes were bright with curiosity.

"No." Margaret eyed her in frustration, weighing how much to say. Clearly, the less said, the better. "It was an accident. He fell in the quarry and drowned." Caitlin's eyes widened and her small mouth fell open, and Margaret quickly said, "I told you it was dangerous. You're not to go anywhere near it unless I'm with you."

Caitlin whipped out her notebook and pencil. She flipped a few pages and asked, "Who drowned?"

Margaret gave up, realizing there was no contest. Caitlin wouldn't be satisfied until she got the whole story out of her. Or thought she had. "Mrs. Knox's handyman."

"Was that who came to the door last night?"

Margaret frowned. "Nobody came to the door last night."

"Yes, they did." Caitlin gave her a long look. "Somebody was yelling and banging on the door. You told him to go away. It was after I went to bed. You were yelling real loud. You woke me up."

"It was just someone on the road who was lost." This sounded like a transparent lie, even to Margaret, and she walked past Caitlin's unblinking stare with the definite feeling that this wasn't the end of it as far as her niece was concerned—not by a long shot.

BY NOON everything in the house shone—the woodwork gleamed, the bathrooms, the piano, the delicately carved legs of the settee in the living room. She vacuumed the floors and rugs, plumped the pillows, dusted, straightened the pictures, washed, dried and folded the laundry.

She was exhausted. All she wanted to do was climb into bed and pull the covers up over her head, but she knew what she would see in her mind's eye—the flat rock, herself pulling Vern Boyce from the quarry. His dead, staring eyes.

Finally she dragged herself to the kitchen and fixed lunch. The hamburgers and fries she cooked were overdone, practically fried to a crisp, but Caitlin ate hers without comment, too intent on her own thoughts to notice what she was eating. Margaret knew she was planning a new assault in her campaign to find out all she could about Vern Boyce's drowning, but hadn't yet figured out the right strategy.

Margaret sat down with a weary sigh and had scarcely swallowed a cup of coffee when the phone rang.

"What's going on up there?" Jake asked peremptorily. "It's all over town that someone's died up at the quarry."

She hesitated. Caitlin seemed engrossed in her French fries, but she was listening to every word. "Yes," she said at last. "Mrs. Knox's handyman, that man who was here, drunk and yelling threats... drowned in the quarry."

"Are you and Caitlin all right?"

Her heart thudded. "Yes, we're both fine."

"Look, I'm tied up for the rest of the afternoon, then I'm coming up there. I can make it around six. We could go out to dinner. If you can't get a sitter for Caitlin, we could eat at the house."

"I'm not much of a cook," she admitted.

"Okay, then I'll do the cooking. I'll be there by six."

She hung up with a sense of physical shock. For some reason, her heart, her breath, every nerve seemed painfully alive, aware, racing, anticipating seeing him again.

Chapter Seven

"What about your promise?" Caitlin demanded suddenly. "You said when the car got fixed, you'd take me someplace special."

Margaret sighed, sensing a battle of wills. "You were supposed to clean your room. It looks like a pigpen."

"That's because I'm decorating," Caitlin replied nonchalantly. "It's supposed to look like that."

"If you want to go someplace special, you have to pick up those toys. A pigpen doesn't make it with me." There was no answer from Caitlin who was sitting on the rug, her head bent over a picture she was coloring. Margaret drew a frustrated breath and picked up a magazine, listing various attractions around Vermont. She leafed through it and stopped, her eye caught by one particular article. There was more than one way to skin a cat. She said, "Caitlin, would you like to see how they make maple syrup in a sugar house? All you have to do is clean your room."

"Okay," she said, glancing up. "Only I need some new magic markers. Could we get some while we're out?"

"Maybe." Vaguely Margaret wondered what had happened to the practically new markers she already had.

Caitlin closed her coloring book. "What's a sugar house?"

"A special place, wait and see." Margaret helped her into a sweater, only half listening as Caitlin's head popped up through the neck.

"In olden days people didn't have markers. They wrote with other stuff, like reg'lar pens. Their writing was funny looking. All squiggly." She grinned up at Margaret. "My markers are real neat. Only they got used up in my picture. Especially the blue one. I needed lots of blue."

"Oh." Margaret glanced in the hall mirror. It was an old mirror, and the wavy, silvery glass made her face look bloodless and pale. She fished in her purse for her lipstick.

"It got all used up. The blue one," Caitlin repeated.

"Uh-huh."

"Well, I need more *blue.*"

"Fine." Margaret put the lipstick back in her purse. "We'll get more while we're out."

"Because I really need them or I can't finish my picture. Want to see it?"

Margaret started to say yes but thought better of it. Caitlin had the most incredible one-track mind. From ten feet away, her picture looked suspiciously like a large body of water with a stick figure of a man in it, floating facedown.

She propelled Caitlin toward the stairs. "Clean your room. Now." Five minutes later Caitlin came down, saying she was ready to go, her room was all clean. Margaret suspected she'd simply moved everything from one flat surface to another. On the other hand, maybe Caitlin had picked it all up. And pigs could fly, she thought morosely. Well, a little trust once in a while wouldn't hurt. Even with Caitlin.

"Okay, let's go," she told her, and Caitlin jumped down the last stair with a yelp of glee and ran outside to the car. Margaret stood motionless in the doorway for a long moment, wondering just what she'd let herself in for. Then she followed her outside.

Today was probably one of the worst days in her life. Margaret couldn't believe that watching Caitlin was turning into a nightmare. Every time she thought about Vern Boyce, she felt like fainting. Hopefully, taking Caitlin maple sugaring would be relaxing and fun. On second thought, nothing could be calming with her niece.

Margaret took the magazine with her. The list of sugar bush camps was fairly comprehensive; the directions to the nearest—Top O' the Hill Farm—two miles north on Route 100.

They found the farm with no problem. It was off a side road, a fair distance up a steep and rolling hillside. As they drove up, a gray-haired man in overalls was just starting a tractor.

"Everett Davis," he said with a welcoming grin. "You're just in time. I'm heading out to the sugar house. Want a ride?"

Margaret shook his hand and introduced herself and Caitlin. "I should have called first, but we stopped by, hoping you'd be sugaring."

His smile widened. "Sure am, and it so happens I need an expert taster." He reached out a hand and gently tousled Caitlin's hair. "How'd you like to volunteer, young lady?"

"Yes, please," she said happily, and in seconds they were seated in back of the tractor, bumping over a makeshift road through the woods.

"Most places use vacuum tubing. It's quicker," Everett Davis shouted over the engine roar. "But I kinda like the ping of sap droppin' in buckets." Winking at Caitlin, he went on, "Besides, squirrels ate most of the danged tubing first year I tried it."

The road wound upward a quarter mile through the woods until at last they arrived at the sugar house, tucked into a stand of old maples with about forty cords of wood stacked neatly in back. A plume of steam issued from the chimney. They got out, and Everett Davis led them inside.

Caitlin twitched her small nose in delight. It was magic. Everything smelled so good, and she got to sample homemade donuts with maple sprinkles on top. She chewed a second donut and looked at the three flat evaporators that filled most of the sugar house. "We add sap to one side," Everett Davis explained. "And we strain what comes out the other end." He grinned at Caitlin. "How about some cider?"

A large barrel with a tap stood in one corner. Everett gave her a mug and told her to help herself; and shortly Caitlin, her stomach full, was peering out the window, hoping to catch a glimpse of deer.

Margaret sat on a stool and sipped instant coffee made with hot sap directly from the evaporator. It was wonderful, relaxing, and best of all, a world away from Quarry Farm and dead bodies. Smiling gratefully at her host, she said, "This is really special."

"It's a lot of work. I've got five sons and two daughters, and everyone pitches in. I planted some of these maples forty years ago. Those trees are youngsters compared to the big ones. Generally I use a team of Belgian horses to collect the sap. Got four teams, nothin' beats 'em." He grinned. "They stop and go on command and don't tear the woods up like a tractor."

Caitlin peered from the window. Something moved outside in the late afternoon gloom. She squinted harder. A breeze had sprung up. Prob'ly just wind blowing the bushes, she thought with a sigh.

Then it moved again. She saw it this time. A big deer with antlers, and a smaller one . . . no, two more standing in the trees. The smallest just a shadow, a light fawn-colored smudge on the blue-black stand of trees. Suddenly they looked up, ears pricked. Then they were gone, bounding away with a flick of white.

Turning from the window, she sighed happily and said, "I saw *three* deers! Just like Bambi!"

Everett laughed and added more wood to the fire in the stove. "Thought I'd seen one earlier today. A big buck."

"No, there were *three. I saw them!*" Caitlin's face was flushed with triumph, and Margaret's heart gave a queer, painful lurch. Caitlin had her dad's mop of light brown curls and a funny turned-up nose, but her stubbornness reminded Margaret irresistibly of herself at that age.

She got up and looked out the window. "They're gone now."

"I know." Caitlin leaned against the wall, arms crossed, prepared to stand there for the rest of the afternoon. "We can wait till they come back."

"We can't do that, honey," she said with a wry smile. "Mr. Davis has other things to do. We're probably holding him up."

Everett looked up from stoking the fire. "Don't let that worry you. I don't have a set schedule. Take your time."

She glanced at her watch. "Actually, we have to get home soon. But we'd love to buy some maple syrup if you've got some for sale."

Happily, he did. And soon they were driving home laden with maple butter and several jugs of home-made syrup, which, Caitlin informed Margaret, she was going to pour on crackers and eat for dinner.

"Okay, but not for dinner, for dessert," Margaret suggested. She would have left it at that, but Caitlin peppered her with complaints, stating that she hated stuff that was good for her.

"It's not fair," Caitlin said grumpily.

"You'd get sick of sweets if that's all you ate."

"No, I wouldn't."

"Would I lie to you?" Margaret insisted, pulling the Fiat to a stop in front of the barn. She turned off the engine and took out the key.

"People don't always tell the truth." Caitlin opened the car door and got out. She gave Margaret a long look. "Robert doesn't."

Oh, no, not that again, Margaret thought. The telephone incident. She frowned and said, "You must have misunderstood what he was doing. I'm sure he called the doctor."

Caitlin followed her into the house. "He didn't. He's a big, fat liar and *I hate him.*"

Margaret put down her purse, nerving herself for another unpleasant argument, but Caitlin disappeared upstairs, and then the phone rang.

It was Sandy. Margaret breathed a sigh of relief. "You don't know how worried I've been. It's been days—"

"I know, and I'm sorry, really. It's just that it's been so hectic. We've been driving around, seeing the sights—wait, Robert wants to say hello."

"Hi, Maggie." Robert's cheery voice boomed on the other end of the line. "How're you doing? How's Cait?"

"We're both fine."

Dimly Margaret heard Sandy's voice in the background. "Give me back the phone..." The sentence ended on a smothered burst of laughter, and Robert continued, "I've got to hang up. We're at a gas station, and some guy wants to use the phone. Everything's fine, right? Bye, Maggie. We'll give you another call in a couple of days."

"No, wait! Something's—" The phone went dead, cutting off Margaret's barely voiced protest. Lips tightly set, she replaced the receiver. God, it was just like him, to talk for two minutes, if that, and not give her a chance to say anything. Damn Robert.

Still annoyed, she turned and saw a pair of headlights edge up the drive. It was Jake. Unconsciously her breath caught in her throat. Thank God he was here.

When she opened the door, he took one look at her face, told her she looked terrible and took her in his arms.

She managed a small smile and said, "Finding Vern Boyce in the quarry this morning took its toll on me." He held her gently. Expressing sympathy, as a friend, her mind warned. But she was pressed so close to him she couldn't move, and she didn't want to move.

His face against her black hair, he kissed her temple and said, "Is there a drink in this place?"

"Oh, Jake." She put her head on his shoulder and swallowed a curious giggle that bubbled in her throat.

He lifted her face and kissed her for a long time. "Now go get us both a drink."

There was bourbon in a decanter on a tray in the living room. Jake splashed some in a glass, added a little water and handed it to her. Then he poured a drink for himself and gave her an encouraging push toward the settee. "Go on, sit down before you fall down."

The drink really gave her a jolt. She knew she was suffering from some sort of post-stress syndrome, delayed shock. She took a deep breath and said, "I'm not the fainting type."

"You look like your knees are going to fold up. Your face was white as a sheet when you answered the door. Now your face is red." He took the glass away from her and put it on the table. "Now tell me what's upsetting you, besides finding the body."

Her throat stung from the bourbon. She took another breath and pulled herself together. "Vern Boyce showed up here late last night, drunk, demanding money. I didn't let him in, and he got angry, shouting threats, pounding on the door. I kept telling him to go away, but he wouldn't. Then a car came along, and he seemed to know who it was. He went to talk to the driver, and that's the last I saw of him—until I found him in the quarry this morning.''

"Did you explain all this to the police?" he asked quietly.

She nodded. "Yes, they said he might have run out of gas. His truck was parked down the road, the keys still in it. The theory is that he stopped here to use the phone, but—"

"But what?"

"He never mentioned wanting to use the phone. He just pounded on the door, yelling things that made no sense." She chewed on her lower lip for a moment, then said with a shrug, "Ranting and raving something about a black fog and how I didn't scare him.''

"Sounds like he was paranoid."

She shrugged again. "He was drunk. I was scared half out of my mind. Then I tried calling the police again, but the line was down. When I looked out the window he was gone, and so was the car."

"What time did this happen?" Jake asked, leaning forward.

"I don't know, after ten-thirty." After a moment she added uncertainly, "No, I ran to call the police, and the clock chimed. It was a little after eleven."

Jake was silent for a moment, then said, "And Vern ended up in the quarry."

"But why would he go up there at that time of night?" she asked, puzzled. "It's too cold to go swimming."

GET 4 BOOKS

FREE

Return this card, and we'll send you 4 brand-new Harlequin Intrigue® novels, absolutely *FREE!* We'll even pay the postage both ways!

We're making you this offer to introduce you to the benefits of the Harlequin Reader Service®: free home delivery of brand-new romance novels, **AND** at a saving of 40¢ apiece compared to the cover price!

Accepting these 4 free books places you under no obligation to continue. You may cancel at any time, even just after receiving your free shipment. If you do not cancel, every month we'll send 4 more Harlequin Intrigue novels and bill you just $2.49* apiece—that's all!

Yes! Please send me my 4 free Harlequin Intrigue novels, as explained above.

Name

Address   Apt.

City   State   Zip

181 CIH AGNY (U-H-I-12/92)

Get 4 Books FREE

SEE BACK OF CARD FOR DETAILS

"Maybe he went there with one of his drinking pals. They could have gone up there to tie one on." He eyed Margaret somberly. "Come on, you're thinking something. I can practically hear cogs whirling in that brain of yours. What is it?"

She shook her head, frowning. "I was remembering how angry he was. He saw the car and said something about knowing how to get what he wanted, then he left."

"That settles it then," Jake said firmly. "He recognized a pal, had another couple of beers. I bet the police will find an empty six-pack or two tossed in the field. Once they were half-bombed out of their minds, they wouldn't care how cold it was. One of them probably suggested swimming, and off they went. Or maybe the pal took off, and Boyce wandered up to the quarry and fell in. An unfortunate accident."

"I guess so. The police asked a lot of questions."

"That's their job." He gave her a reassuring smile and said, "What about Caitlin? How's she taking all this?"

"In perfect stride. It's just another mystery for the great detective to solve." Margaret shook her head and went on, "I took her off to a sugar house this afternoon, to get her away from here. We both needed it." She gave him a rueful grin. "Lord knows if it did any good."

Jake gazed at Margaret as her shoulders slumped a little, the cloud of black hair tumbling about her pale face, her slim body in a wine-colored wool dress...she was so damn vulnerable.

A muscle in his jaw tightened. He rose to his feet and moved toward her, then stopped himself. From the stairs came the sound of footsteps, and Caitlin ran into the room. She took one look at Margaret and said loudly, "I'm starved, and you forgot to buy my markers. You promised!"

"I'm sorry," Margaret told her. "Next time I go to town, I promise." Caitlin still looked grumpy, and she added hurriedly, "Your mom and Robert called a few minutes ago. They asked how you were and said to give you their love."

Caitlin hunched her shoulders. "How come I didn't get to talk to Mom?"

"They hung up before I could tell you," she explained. "They were in a gas station, someone else wanted to use the phone." She threw Jake an exasperated look. "I think Robert just ran out of change. You'd think he'd get a telephone credit card, but you know how he feels about credit cards. He absolutely refuses to use them."

"Really? I didn't know—" Jake looked slightly puzzled.

"Well, I'm still hungry," Caitlin announced with a heavy frown.

Jake smiled at her. "Lead me to the kitchen. I'm a genius with leftovers. I'll whip us up something good in no time."

Immediately Caitlin's eyes lit up. "Can I help?"

His grin widened. "Sure."

Rushing into the kitchen, Caitlin dragged a stool up to the counter. "I get to stir, and if there are any eggs, I get to break them."

Margaret followed her into the kitchen and wrapped a large green apron around Caitlin's waist. "You're the official assistant chef." She glanced at Jake and added, "I guess eggs are on the menu."

"Omelets," he replied from the depths of the refrigerator. "There's ham in here, tomatoes, lots of good stuff."

In a matter of minutes, he and Caitlin had prepared a fragrant omelet mixture and poured it in a frying pan while Margaret set the table. Caitlin rushed around the kitchen, fetching various ingredients, dropping only two eggs on the floor—accidents Jake dismissed airily with a grin and a wink.

The two chefs tossed a green salad with Jake's secret dressing, and they sat down to eat. Caitlin, face sticky with maple syrup she'd poured on her omelet, exclaimed after two bites, "It's *great!* Want some syrup? It's real good."

"No, thanks," Margaret and Jake said in chorus.

Caitlin gave them a complacent look, chomped down the rest of her omelet, and burped in a vulgar fashion. "'Scuse me. Can I go upstairs now? I wanna play 'Uncle Wiggly.'" Margaret nodded helplessly, and Caitlin dashed upstairs.

"She's really something else," Jake said with a laugh.

Margaret tilted her head and gave him a warm smile. "What amazes me is that she cleaned her plate without an argument. I can never get her to do anything without a pitched battle."

"Knowing how to handle kids isn't all that hard," he said blandly. "Treat 'em like anyone else. Respect their dignity."

"And feed them delicious suppers," she added with a satisfied sigh. "Your secret salad dressing was wonderful."

He leaned back in his chair, chuckling. "Good food, good company...I'll have you eating out of my hand in no time."

"Not so fast. You have Caitlin right where you want her, but I'm older and wiser."

The grooves that ran from his nose to his chiseled mouth deepened as he laughed. He really had a magic touch with a frying pan, she thought. And with small children, too.

She lifted her eyes and looked across the table at Jake. He was reaching for the carafe of wine, and she stared at the width of his broad shoulders and the beautifully coordinated way he moved. He went to top up her glass, and she put her hand over the rim.

"No, no more, please," she said with a smile. "Another drink, and I'll fall asleep right here. I've no head for alcohol."

He smiled back at her in a way that shimmered down to the very soles of her feet. "Dessert? If you have any fresh fruit, we could have—no, on second thought, I'll take care of that...later."

"Oh, no," she pleaded laughingly. "I couldn't eat another bite." She felt tantalized with food and drink and something else she didn't dare analyze—a feeling lovely and wonderful.

He got up and switched on the stereo, and the strains of a French love song wafted on the air. "Come on, a little exercise will clear your head." He took her in his arms, and Margaret gave in to her base desires and wrapped both arms around his shoulders, more or less draping herself on him.

"Jake, I know I'm not much help, but I can hardly stand, let alone dance. That wine—"

"I'll hold us both up," he said with a laugh. "Let's see if a little passive exercise helps."

She followed him perfectly as they swayed gently from side to side. And when she became aware that her head was resting against his neck, her eyes on a level with the pulse that beat just under his jaw, she felt her breath catch in her throat.

There was a certain tension in the way he was holding her, and she straightened away from him, allowing her arms to assume a more normal position. "Don't move," he whispered, kissing her hair.

"You're terrible, plying me with liquor," she accused, laughter burbling in her husky voice. "And irresistible food, and what was worse, I sat here and let you do it. I didn't stand a chance."

"Maybe I poured the wine, but you sat across the table looking at me with those big, green eyes," he teased. "Those lips." He dropped another kiss on her hair and said softly, "I'm the one who didn't stand a chance."

"Is that so?" She laughed up at him, feeling wonderful, exhilarated, and just a little dizzy.

His feet slowed to a stop and his arms tightened, and she was acutely aware of every muscle in the length of his body. "I think we'll take a rain check on dessert. You're in no condition to appreciate the subtleties of my fresh-fruit compote." He leaned down and kissed her again, savoring the feel of her lips, the sweet taste of her mouth.

By some sleight of hand, which was beyond her comprehension, she found herself lying on the settee half on top of him, her face tucked into the curve of his neck. She breathed in the clean scent of soap and slightly musky maleness, a smile curving her lips. She opened her mouth and tasted the tautness of his skin and felt an immediate reaction beneath her.

"God, Margaret, you're beautiful," he groaned, and his hands did something wonderful to her back. The touch of cool, evening air touched her flesh as the zipper of her dress slid down.

Passion raced through her body, rousing her from her dreamy state, and she pulled away slightly. "Jake, I don't know..."

All her old doubts returned with a rush, and she found herself at war with her own inclinations. She wanted to trust her judgment and fall in love. He seemed so...right. But she'd been terribly wrong about Robert, and her intellect told her it could happen again. There were no guarantees in love. What if he didn't feel the same way she did? What if Jake wasn't interested in a long-term relationship?

His hands moved over the satiny skin of her back and then slipped under her own weight to cup her bare breasts, and she could feel the swollen softness tightening into hard nubs pushing against his palms in an involuntary invitation that left her shaken and breathless.

He turned his face and she was drawn into a kiss that left her open and completely vulnerable, a kiss that sent wild emergency signals racing to all the shadowy feminine areas of her body. And when she felt his hands smoothing her hips, sliding slowly on that bit of nylon that covered her under the fallen sides of her dress, she panicked. His hands were pressing her even closer now, and she began to struggle. "No, please . . . Jake," she pleaded, scrambling up to sit trembling on the edge of the settee. She tugged at her dress, pulling it up over her suddenly chilled shoulders. She fumbled with the zipper and finally got it up. Where were her shoes?

And then the doorbell rang. Jake's smoky gaze met hers and a reluctant grin crept across his face. "Saved by the bell."

She went in her stockinged feet to answer it. A woman was standing on the front porch. She smiled coolly as Margaret opened the door and said in a breathy, slightly flustered voice, "Yes?"

"Ah, I'm Violet Chadwick, a dear friend of Polly Knox's," the woman said, a small smile curving her thin lips. "Polly borrowed a special book of mine a few months ago. I know she's in Europe and it's rather late to be calling, but I tried to telephone you earlier. The line must be out again. This town has terrible phone service." The woman smiled again. "Anyway, I wondered if I might come in and look for that book. It means a great deal to me, and I'm sure Polly wouldn't mind."

Jake came up behind Margaret as she shook her head. "I'm sorry. I can't take responsibility for something like that. You'll have to wait until Mrs. Knox comes back from Europe. I'm really sorry."

Violet Chadwick stiffened. A small woman, she could have been anywhere from thirty to forty, with chiseled lips and glossy black hair. Her eyes were obscured by large, brown-tinted glasses, and she wore a well-cut blue silk suit. She frowned. "I can see you don't quite understand. Really, Polly wouldn't mind."

"Perhaps not," Margaret interrupted sweetly. "The point is, *I would.* I'm sorry, you'll just have to wait. Good night." She closed the door as the woman drew a breath of anger and stalked off the porch toward her car.

Margaret turned to find Jake smiling at her with appreciation. "You handled that with authority. Very impressive." They turned and went back to the living room.

Violet Chadwick got behind the wheel of her car and slammed the door. A rosy splotch spread over her features as she drove off ill-temperedly toward town.

MARGARET CAME UP for air from Jake's teasing kisses. "Who's doing the dishes?"

"You wash, I'll dry," he suggested, nuzzling the side of her neck. "Mmm, you smell delicious." Abruptly the doorbell rang again. For a moment they stood, frozen, staring at each other. Then Jake said, frowning, "Are you expecting anyone else?"

"No." The house was like Grand Central Station, the phone ringing constantly, people banging on the door at all hours of the day and night. Margaret shrugged wearily, and they went back to the front hall. She opened the door.

Madame Zorina stood there, a figure straight out of a Gothic horror movie. She wore a black, hooded cloak that blended with the darkness so that her wrinkled face seemed to float within the dark hood. Over her arm was a basket of vials, bundles of dried herbs and strings of garlic.

"I had to come," she said. "It was my brother you found dead in the quarry. I foretold his death...." She raised a hand to push back her hood, and Margaret saw that she was trembling. Determination and a strange exultation glowed in her eyes.

Margaret opened the door wider. "Why, Madame Zorina, I didn't know...I'm so sorry." Her voice trailed off helplessly. Not knowing what to say, she shook her head and gestured toward Jake. "This is Jake McCall, a friend of mine." He nodded politely but shot Margaret a puzzled glance, obviously startled by the psychic's bizarre appearance.

Madame Zorina stepped into the hallway, her eyes moving quickly, scanning everything. "This house is full of evil. I feel it. Terrible illness, hatred and death. It must be purified," she said finally. "Dark forces are at work. You are in danger, I must weave a circle of protection."

A smile tugged at the corner of Jake's mouth. "Perhaps Madame Zorina would like a drink. I could use one myself."

They moved to the living room, and Jake mixed drinks. He handed the psychic a strong whiskey and water. She drank deeply, then lowered the glass and seemed to get a grip on herself. Settling her bulk into an armchair, she said, "I used my crystal pendulum. It twirls, and the directions it takes indicate answers to questions I put to it. Right means yes, and widdershins, that is, left, means no. Usually." She drew a deep breath and went on, "My brother was a fool."

"Look, madame," Jake said, a faint ghost of suspicion narrowing his eyes, "we're sorry about your brother's death. But it has nothing to do with this house or Margaret. You're wasting your time with all this talk of dark forces."

She drew another deep breath, her eyes fixing him with a glittery, malevolent stare. "You don't believe me. I sense your thoughts, and you're wrong. Dead wrong. You will beg for my help before this is over, and I may not be here to give it."

Jake muttered under his breath, "This is crazy."

Margaret frowned and said, "Madame, why won't you be here? Do you think some harm may come to you, like your brother, Vern?"

"No, certainly not," the psychic retorted, horrified. "I'm well aware of the evil forces my brother tampered with, but my absence will be more mundane. I have reservations for a weekend at Atlantic City. I intend to make a killing at the blackjack tables."

Jake grinned at Margaret conspiratorially. Maybe the psychic was crazy as a loon, but clearly she had her own agenda. And she obviously didn't have any hangups about using her so-called powers for monetary gain.

"I don't claim all the answers, but I have powers," Madame Zorina crooned. "You came here by chance, didn't you, Mr. McCall. You find you're linked to Margaret by strange circumstance. Oh, don't bother answering. I know. I've seen this in the Tarot. You both are linked now and for all time, into death and beyond. You had to come. The golden chain that binds you called you here when Margaret needed you."

Madame Zorina rose, her black skirts whirling about her ankles. Jake let out a long breath. It was possible the psychic had some kind of ESP power. He opened his mouth, but before he could speak, Madame Zorina interrupted. "You couldn't save your sister—even if you'd been in this country when she fell ill. Nothing could've altered the events."

Jake turned and spoke to Margaret. There was a look of compassion in his face as he glanced back at the old woman. "I don't know how she knows about Betsy's death, or that I was out of the country then. There has to be a perfectly logical explanation for all this." He leaned down and kissed Margaret's cheek, saying softly, "Let the old girl work her spells and incantations. Humor her. Later on, I'll drive back to town and get my things. You can't continue to stay on in this nut house by yourself... with only Caitlin for company."

Margaret sagged against him in relief. There was no point in being coy. She *knew* she wanted him to stay at the house, and what's more, he knew it, too. The look of gratitude in her green eyes told him all he needed to know.

Abruptly Madame Zorina rubbed her hands together. "We must begin at once. Time is short, almost the full moon, the time of greatest danger. Protection must be symbolic. Come, we must turn out the lights and use only candles."

Margaret whispered to Jake, "We might as well. It's the fastest way to get rid of her." He shrugged in agreement and switched off the table lamps. Margaret moved about, lighting several candles. In the eerie, moving light, the moon looked uncanny, shrouded in darkness with only the glow of candlelight.

Outside it was raining again. And gradually, as Margaret watched the old woman's face and glittering stare, the rasp of her voice and soft drumming of the rain on the roof blended into a single low sound. Her cramped legs grew numb as she sat in the middle of the rug with Jake. He was half swearing beneath his breath as Madame Zorina began anointing the windows and doors with liquid from the flask she produced from her basket. She walked backward, dribbling the contents of the flask in a wide circle around the seated pair. She was careful to stay within the unbroken circle.

She said to Margaret, "There are emanations in this house. Lies, menace, evil. Hate. I feel it. The scarlet beast, one who uses the silver tongue of the serpent—he is the Evil One. And he is not alone. There is another who seeks to harm you and the child." Suddenly her eyes darted toward the stairs.

Caitlin was standing there, rubbing her eyes sleepily. "How come you turned off the lights? What are you doing?"

Madame Zorina whirled, and again her inky skirts flared outward. She pointed a clawlike finger at Caitlin. "Don't worry, child. I have said you are the catalyst, and so you shall be. No power on earth can change your destiny. You will save the ones you love."

Chapter Eight

Madame Zorina walked toward Caitlin, holding out a string of garlic like a Hawaiian lei. Margaret ran past her and put her arms around Caitlin. "Please leave her out of this." Turning to Caitlin she said firmly, "You're supposed to be in bed."

The psychic went over to the doorway and began draping the garlic across the lintel. Fascinated, Caitlin couldn't take her eyes off her. "Gosh, she's real neat! And she says I'm gonna save everyone!"

"We don't need to be saved," Margaret muttered, marching her niece toward the stairs. "It's your bedtime. Madame's upset. Her brother just died."

Caitlin scowled. "Nancy's mom says she's schizofrantic. If I had a brother and he died, I'd be schizofrantic, too. How come he died?"

"Her brother was Vern Boyce, the man who drowned in the quarry," Margaret admitted tiredly. "Come on, up you go. Back to bed."

Caitlin's scowl deepened and she stubbornly refused to budge. "I want to stay and watch. How come she's putting all that stinky stuff on the doors?"

"It's garlic. She thinks the house is unhappy and, er, needs to have its bad feelings removed." Margaret hauled her up another stair.

Caitlin's eyes widened. "Like that movie where there were ghosts in the TV and everyone disappeared in a hole in the closet? Wow! Maybe we have ghosts!"

"We don't have any ghosts," Margaret retorted, glancing over her shoulder at Madame Zorina who was fingering her crystal and pointing it at Caitlin with an unnerving fixed stare. She was also mumbling under her breath, reeling off a litany of spells.

"Ackshully, we do have ghosts," Caitlin said complacently. "Madame Zorina's brother's prob'ly a ghost now, and he's real mad because he drowned. The ghosts in that movie were angry. They came right up where they were digging a swimming pool. Maybe her brother's gonna come out of the quarry like that and get us!" She looked up at Margaret, and her expression was just what Margaret expected it would be—excitement and delight overlaid by a thin glaze of fright.

Margaret dropped a kiss on Caitlin's forehead and hugged her tight. "No one's going to get us. Vern Boyce isn't there anymore, honey. The police came and took him away in the ambulance."

"But the quarry could still have lots of skeletons," Caitlin said hopefully. "Mrs. Knox and other people Robert decided to get rid of. That's prob'ly where he hides all the bodies."

She stared at Caitlin, at a complete loss for words, and Jake came to the rescue. "Interesting theory. We'll have to discuss it in the morning. Hang on, I'll give you a piggy-back ride up to bed." He hoisted Caitlin up on his shoulders and took her upstairs before she could protest. Then Margaret heard his voice telling Caitlin he would read her a story if she promised to go right to bed. And of course Caitlin demanded one with a ghost in it. "I don't know any," Jake said, faint amusement evident in his voice.

Margaret leaned against the banister. He sounded so comfortable, so calm. She felt her frazzled nerve ends begin to smooth out. After all, why should she be so uptight? Compared to Vern Boyce, she had little to complain about.

Madame Zorina came into the hall, shrugging into her cloak. "I did what I could, but it may not be enough." Her wrinkled face was lined with worry. "Remember my warning. Beware of the time of the full moon and be careful around water. One more caution—the serpent glides in *deadly* earnest. I have seen him in visions. You will have to defeat him." Then she stamped out of the house, leaving a silence that vibrated.

Jake came downstairs. "My God," he said faintly. "Madame Zorina's really something, isn't she? No doubt flying home on her broomstick."

Margaret straightened away from the banister. "At this point, nothing would surprise me."

He looked out the window as he shrugged into his raincoat. "Nope, there goes her car down the road. No broomstick." He opened the door, and their eyes met. "Forget Madame Zorina's nonsense, and stop worrying about her brother's death. He was drunk and fell in the quarry."

She sighed tiredly. "I guess you're right. I'm worrying about nothing."

They stood in silence for a few seconds, then Jake pulled her into his arms and kissed her long and hard. "Lock the door behind me. I'll be back as soon as I can."

After he'd gone she went back to the living room and switched on the table lamps, then put out the candles, one by one. She got a broom and swept up the neat little piles of herbs Madame Zorina had dribbled on the floor. Then she went to the kitchen and put the kettle on. When the water boiled, she made a mug of tea and sat drinking it with one eye on the kitchen clock, waiting for Jake to return. The tea was scorching hot, but she sipped it absently.

Madame Zorina's voice echoed in her mind. "This house is evil and full of lies."

She stirred the tea and then paused, the spoon dripping unnoticed onto her dress as her mind grappled with that ugly thought. This house, nestled cozily on a mountain, with bucolic hayfields tumbling down to the valley below, was just a simple Vermont farmhouse. Nothing sinister or evil about it . . . except that Vern Boyce had drowned in the quarry. *Stop it,* Margaret told herself. That was just an accident.

Some imp of perversity reminded her Caitlin had talked about lies . . . *Robert's lies.*

Ridiculous, she thought. Believing everything a seven-year-old said was on a par with believing Madame Zorina.

The doorbell rang again, startling her. Margaret jumped and noticed the puddle of tea on her dress. She put the spoon back in the mug and mopped disgustedly at the spot with a napkin. Not much good, but it didn't matter. Jake was back. And she realized for the moment that was all that mattered.

THE LIGHTS FLICKERED as she unlocked the front door. Outside the downpour was deafening, like a solid wall of water beyond the porch. Jake's dark hair was plastered flat to his head; the ends dripped water. The shoulders of his tan trench coat were black with rain. As he shrugged it off, the overhead chandelier chose that moment to flicker ominously again. It was symptomatic of the state of Margaret's nerves that she jumped like a nervous rabbit.

"Maybe a bad bulb," he said, looking up at the chandelier with a frown.

"No, the hall lights dimmed a minute ago, too. I hope we're not in for a power outage." She draped his coat on the umbrella stand.

"So we keep this handy." He grinned and picked up a candle. "Come on, I'll make coffee. Something hot. You're white as a sheet."

Her face was pale and drawn, her eyes huge with exhaustion, and she was shivering. There'd been a chill draft when the front door had been open, but it was closed now, and she was still shaking. The lights flickered again, then went out altogether. Jake fumbled with matches and lit the candle. He smiled at her across the flame. "Ah, let there be light."

"I'm so glad you're staying," she said fervently, moving closer. He slid his free arm around her and they went out to the kitchen. He told her to sit while he made coffee.

He dried his wet head with a dish towel and got down two mugs. His movements in the murky darkness were accompanied with bumps and repressed exclamations. He was limping slightly as he carried the kettle over to the table and poured hot water into the mugs.

"I took my shoes off and then kept stubbing my toe." He grinned apologetically as she glanced at his stockinged feet.

"We're a matched pair. My shoes are somewhere in the living room." She warmed herself with the glow of his smile. The color began to come back into her face.

"I like candlelight. It's romantic, even worth my clumsiness." His eyes twinkled endearingly, making her laugh.

She wished she could simply enjoy his company instead of having to worry about bodies, weird psychics and Caitlin, who spent most of her time making wild accusations about her stepfather. Robert was a lot of things, she thought. But he wasn't a criminal or a liar.

Even though she'd already had a cup of tea, the coffee tasted good. Her mind felt clearer. Robert had told one lie she knew of. He'd denied ever having been in this house before renting it, and the snapshot in Caitlin's shoebox proved that wasn't true.

Her quick smile faded, leaving her pensive looking. Jake stared at her for a long moment. "Funny, you look a little like my sister in this light. Betsy had dark hair, too. Her birthday's next Thursday." He drew a breath and said, "She would have been twenty-six if she'd lived."

"It's so sad. She had everything to live for, youth, a loving husband." Margaret murmured.

"And no money problems. No small thing in this day and age," he said with a shrug. "Betsy had a hefty trust fund from her godmother." Getting to his feet, he hauled her out of the chair. "You look all in. Go on up to bed."

There was another candlestick on the small table by the stairs. He lighted it with his candle, handed it to her, and they went upstairs. "This bedroom is yours," she said, opening the door. "The bathroom's just down the hall. If you need another blanket, the linen closet's next door." She smiled and saw a subtle response in his eyes.

There was a laughing note in his voice as he said, "I won't need another blanket. I'm pretty warm-blooded." His smile turned into a devilish grin.

She reminded herself Caitlin was sleeping not twenty feet down the hall. That is, if she was really asleep. Margaret opened her own bedroom door and placed her candle on the bedside table. Turning, she looked over her shoulder at Jake. "Good night."

"You're beautiful," he said, watching her flush. He looked as if he was about to say something else, but changed his mind, and instead, just stood looking at her.

I'm falling in love with you, Margaret. The words formed themselves in *her* mind as he watched her with twinkling eyes. Seven words so clear that for a moment she thought he'd said them aloud. She stared at him, overwhelmed. The laughter was gone from his blue-gray eyes now, and she couldn't decide what expression was in its place. All she knew was that she'd heard those wonderful seven words in her head, and there he was, watching her with a gentle and perceptive glint in his eyes.

"I want—" she mumbled helplessly. "I...I don't know what I want." In two swift strides Jake was standing in front of her. He pulled her gently against his chest and slid both arms around her waist. His hands moved gently upward, caressing her back to her shoulders. She could feel the strength of his arms and the warmth of his passion and had just enough time to close her lips shut before his mouth covered hers.

His lips were warm and hard. She denied the sudden unexpected tingling in her own body and clenched her hands at her sides so she couldn't throw both arms around his neck and give herself to his embrace completely. He drew her even closer, his tongue flicking along her full lower lips, teasing into the corners.

She forced herself not to respond, feeling her nails dig into her palms as she stood rock still.

He lifted his mouth from hers, and with his face still close said the seven words aloud. "I'm falling in love with you, Margaret. Think about that tonight while I'm sleeping down the hall in my lonely bed." Then he leaned down and kissed her cheeks, her eyelids and lastly her forehead. "You haunt me, darling, but I can wait until you're ready."

She lifted her arms and ran her open palms across his taut chest, feeling the smooth muscles beneath his shirt. Their eyes met, and she smiled. Somehow it seemed that he moved an inch closer, and her heart lurched at the gentle light she saw there in his eyes.

"Good night, sweetheart," he whispered, pushing her inside her bedroom. "Before I change my mind."

"Good night," she said in a strangled voice as the door closed softly. She undressed by candlelight, pulled a nightgown over her head and crawled into bed. For five long minutes she lay there, staring at the ceiling, listening to rain falling on the roof, fighting the urge to go down the hall and knock on his door.

Finally she admitted it was a losing battle and got out of bed again. She padded barefoot down the hall and knocked softly. "Hi," she said in a small voice as he opened the door. "I...I couldn't sleep. I thought maybe you'd still be up."

He gave her a steady look. "What did you have in mind? Cards?"

"No."

"Then what do you want?" A dimple lurked in his right cheek.

Margaret answered with her eyes, and Jake hesitated only a moment before scooping her up in his arms. "I've been lying in bed staring at the ceiling, and all I see is you," he said thickly, kissing her lingeringly on her mouth. "You're shivering. We'd better get you straight to bed."

She slid her arms around his neck. "I'm getting warmer, but I'm still cold. I think I need drastic treatment."

He grinned broadly, carried her into his room and kicked the door shut. Their laughter and bantering came to a halt as their eyes locked. Jake laid her down gently on the bed. "Are you sure this is what you want?" He still held her in his arms, sliding one hand into her hair. He curved his other hand around her face and caressed her cheek with his thumb.

"Yes, I'm sure," she said hoarsely, not averting her eyes, and intensely aware with every fiber of her body that she wanted him.

He kissed her gently, then lifted his head slightly. "What about Caitlin? Is this going to be awkward for you?"

Margaret shook her head. "No, she's asleep. And the truth is, I wanted you to stay. I was almost afraid to stay alone with her in the house with everything that's happened." Her breath brushed his lips, and she felt sweet, honeyed passion flow through her. Her eyes met his in an intense gaze. "This feels so right...so wonderful, Jake. I need you. I can't think straight when you touch me."

"Sweetheart, what do you think touching you does to me?" He lowered his mouth that remaining fraction of an inch, kissing her deeply as he lay beside her.

She surrendered completely to the spell of his nearness, lost in sensation as he pulled her nightgown off. Afterward, he settled his hands gently on her hips and pulled her against him. "I want to make love, darling."

She let out a long sigh of delight. "So do I." She parted her lips as his grazed hers, his tongue flicking inside her mouth. His hands slid upward, shaping the slimness of her waist, upward...and she felt her breasts swell in anticipation of his touch. Pulling her tongue from his mouth, she kissed his lips, featherlight, slow, just brushing them with hers. Then she sank her head on his warm shoulder, drifting in the tantalizing pull of passion, feeling her naked body against his hard length.

Her eyes closed as his fingers twined in her hair at the back of her neck, caressing, turning her face up to his as he came up between her legs. He was gentle at first, slowly, inexorably moving inside her. Her arms were around him, palms flat on the damp, warm skin of his back. Holding him, aware of every sinewy muscle, every hard plane of his body.

He whispered into her hair, "Oh yes, darling, that feels so good." He pulled her tightly to him as she kissed him, their bodies moved in timeless rhythm.

He was driving her insane with pleasure and longing, and what had been calm and tender erupted into unchained passion. Her mind emptied, and she knew nothing but the explosive heat of his body throbbing into hers.

Afterward they lay together for a long time, not speaking.

He touched her cheek with his fingertips. "That was wonderful. Oh, my darling..."

She smiled, perfectly content. This wasn't just a passing, thrilling sexual encounter. It was something more than the physical act of love. He was all she'd ever dreamed of in a man, all she'd ever wanted. Her eyelids drooped, her breathing deepened, and she slept in his arms.

He lay beside her, not moving, not wanting to disturb the deep sleep into which she'd drifted. She felt so soft. He held her close and brushed her face with his lips. Her skin felt like warm silk.

He gazed down at her in the candlelight's glow. She lay curled within his arm, her body nestled close. Protect and love, for better or worse, until death—

She must have heard his small intake of breath. She opened her eyes, saying, "I'm not asleep." Turning sideways, she drew him closer, sliding her arm over his body.

"What do you say we try that again?" His voice was a throaty whisper, then his lips came down on hers as the candle flame guttered out and the room fell into darkness. Rain drummed softly on the roof, but neither noticed.

Chapter Nine

Warm lips brushed hers. The touch was a butterfly kiss. Margaret drew a deep breath and opened her eyes to find Jake smiling down at her. He leaned over and kissed her again. "Mmm," she breathed, placing her hands on his shoulders, drawing him close. Something sweet and wonderful was exploding inside her, and she kissed him slowly, deeply, unable to find words to explain how she felt.

He rolled over, the light in his eyes asking, demanding, and she smiled up into his intense gaze. He was so close his breath fanned her cheek. "Oh, Jake..." Her voice trailed off in a happy sigh. She reached up to pull him nearer and abruptly froze.

From down the hall Caitlin's voice yelled, *"Maarrgarret!"*

She sat up, the sheet sliding down to uncover her breasts, and Jake's breath caught in a sigh of regret. He groaned and rolled over. "Talk about poor timing."

"Sounds like she's sick." Margaret slipped out of bed and pulled on her nightgown as Caitlin began coughing plaintively. "Maybe after I give her some

medicine, she'll go back to sleep and you and I can do
something more interesting.''

UNFORTUNATELY the rest of Margaret's morning
passed in a blur. Caitlin's throat ached, her nose was
stuffed up and her eyes were red. When Margaret took
her temperature, she had a slight fever.

Jake had just finished taking a shower when she
passed him in the hall outside Caitlin's room. He wore
a white towel around his waist, his naked back was
dark and lean, beaded with droplets of water. Dancing rays of sunlight from the hall window caught in his
wet hair, and she forgot everything but the need to be
in his arms. He bent his head and kissed her. His lips
tasted wet from his shower. He smelled clean and
soapy and faintly masculine. She kissed him back
whole-heartedly.

Caitlin's loud wailing brought her back to reality.
''I've got to give her more cough medicine,'' Margaret sighed. Jake suggested he needed a certain kind
of medicine, and she laughed, ''Maybe later.''

''MARGARET, I'm thirsty!'' Caitlin wailed for the
tenth time that morning. ''I want a popsicle.''

She poked her head around Caitlin's door. ''Okay,
okay, keep your shirt on. You can have a popsicle after you take a spoonful of this syrup.''

Caitlin heaved herself up among the pillows. ''I said
I need a popsicle. Didn't you hear me?'' Another violent heave and she knocked over a pile of comics,
which slid off the bed and onto the floor. Tumbled in
the mess was a small wooden box.

"Yes, I heard you," Margaret said between clenched teeth, bending to pick it all up. With the box in her hands she looked at Caitlin. "Where did you get this? You haven't been in Mrs. Knox's room again, have you?"

"No, you said not to. I found it in the attic, in a trunk with some old clothes."

Margaret tugged at the lid, but the box wouldn't open. "You're not supposed to play in the attic." Curious, she asked, "What's in it?"

"Some dumb old papers. It had my name on it. I'll show you how it works. It's a puzzle box." Caitlin pressed her fingers on the design of wooden inlaid squares. When the lid opened, she took out the papers.

"This isn't your name, honey. It's Great-Aunt Caitlin's." Margaret scanned the papers...and couldn't believe what she saw on one of them. Shaking, she put the other papers back in the box and numbly held on to the one she left out. She forced herself to look at the paper again. It was a business contract with Great-Aunt Caitlin's name on it...and one other signature...that of a nurse, Polly Merrill.

Stunned for a moment, Margaret put it down and picked up the cough syrup.

"How come she has my name?" Caitlin asked suspiciously.

"It's a family name. Your mom named you after Great-Aunt Caitlin. Now open your mouth." Margaret poked a spoonful of cough syrup into her mouth. "I'll get that popsicle for you."

"I can't breathe." Caitlin sniffled loudly. "Am I gonna die?"

"No, you're tougher than this cold. You'll be fine." Margaret noticed the glass thermometer had slid down among the blanket folds and reached for it just as Caitlin sat on it. Caitlin handed her the two pieces and flopped back on the pillows, managing to look weak and pathetically helpless.

Margaret sighed. "Now I'll have to find another thermometer."

"There's another one in the table next to Mom's bed," Caitlin said in a small voice. "I know because I was looking in the drawer for something ... a pair of scissors, and it was next to some of Mom's wedding pictures."

Margaret went down the hall to Sandy and Robert's room to get the thermometer, but her mind was still on the piece of paper she'd found in her aunt's box. Things were becoming very bizarre. She just wanted to block everything out of her mind.

She opened the door to her sister's room and went to the bedside table drawer. Pulling the drawer open, Margaret found what she was looking for. Unable to resist, she took Sandy and Robert's wedding pictures out and began skimming through them. There was a snapshot of the two as they left the church. And there, behind and just to the left was a woman with blond hair—who looked like the same person in the snapshot in Mrs. Knox's dressing table, which had to be Mrs. Knox herself. She wore a dark blue suit, pearls and sparkling earrings in this picture. And she was staring at Robert with an odd expression on her face. The earrings...Margaret drew a long breath of shock and took the picture over to the window where the light was better. Then she went to Sandy's jewelry case and took out the earring Jake had found. When she took it back to the window and compared it to the ones Mrs. Knox was wearing in the snapshot, she went numb.

Trying to clear her head in order to think, Margaret started to piece everything together. Jake found an earring in Robert's car, which Margaret assumed was Sandy's. Then the woman in the snapshot—who had to be Mrs. Knox—was wearing the same earring. And to further complicate matters, Caitlin said she'd read a letter from Robert to Mrs. Knox, which he'd signed *love*.

The only logical explanation—and one she just couldn't believe—was that Robert and Mrs. Knox had been lovers! And somehow Robert had ended up renting her house after he'd married Sandy. What a mess....

"Aunt Maarrgarret, where are you? I'm hungry! I want a popsicle!" Caitlin's voice floated querulously down the hall.

Startled, Margaret stuffed the snapshot and earring in her pocket and went back to Caitlin's room. Her niece glared up from behind her comic book. "Where's my popsicle? I need it right now."

"First, young lady, I'm going to take your temperature." Margaret took advantage of Caitlin's open mouth to stick the thermometer inside. After a minute she took it out; it read just under one hundred degrees. "Drink some juice, and I'll go get your popsicle."

Caitlin glared but did as she was told, sitting up to finish the juice while Margaret straightened the bed and smoothed the sheets. And there, sticking out from under the pillow next to her ever-present notebook, was an envelope. Margaret picked it up. It was unsealed. Inside was a small white pill. She frowned at Caitlin, who flopped back on the pillows and began coughing loudly.

"Where did this come from?" She turned the envelope over. Nothing was written on it. "Where did you get this?" She stared at Caitlin, determined to get an answer out of her, one way or another.

Caitlin glowered at her. "I found it in the drawer by Mom's bed. I bet Robert was giving her stuff to make her sick. Bugs or something. I hate him! He's mean! He caught me coming out of their room and he twisted my arm, an Indian burn, and said that's what happened to kids who stuck their noses where they didn't belong. He stinks!"

Margaret sighed. "What am I going to do with you? You never should have touched this."

"There's lots more medicine. It's not like that's all there was. Robert was always giving Mom stuff to take. And she kept throwing up. Anyways, it was only one dumb pill." Caitlin made a face. "I only wanted to see what it was, like if he put bugs or worms in it to make her throw up."

"Margaret," Jake called from the foot of the stairs. "The eggs are done. I'll get the morning paper." The front door closed, and he went down the driveway to the mailbox.

Margaret had forgotten that Jake was making breakfast. "This isn't the end of this," she said firmly, waving the envelope with the capsule in it at Caitlin. "I'm going downstairs, but we'll discuss this later." She started downstairs, debating what to do. It was after nine o'clock, Sandy's doctor's office should be open. She ought to call and see if he could fit Caitlin in without an appointment. That would put to rest any fear that she was sick with anything more serious than a cold.

She found the paper in the hall table with emergency numbers written on it and dialed the doctor's number just as Jake came in, shutting the front door behind him.

He eyed her curiously. "Who're you calling?"

"Sandy's doctor," she said. "I'd like him to take a look at Caitlin. Would you get her a popsicle? Grape, if possible."

He nodded, dropped a kiss on her nose and went out to the kitchen. A minute later, flourishing a purple popsicle, he went upstairs.

He knocked on Caitlin's door. "Hi. Heard you were hungry."

"Goody, grape!" Caitlin wriggled with pleasure, ripped off the wrapper, and stuck it in her mouth.

"How about some company?" He sat down on the side of the bed, pushing aside a clutter of games and comics. "Not feeling so good, hmm?"

"Awful." Caitlin sniffed pathetically and eyed him over the popsicle. "And Aunt Margaret's real mad. She won't listen, and it's not fair. It's not my fault."

He gave her an encouraging smile. "She's pretty fair-minded. Just talk to her. It can't be that bad."

"Yes, it is." She munched on the popsicle. "Besides, it's all Robert's fault."

"He's not even here. What's Robert got to do with your aunt's being mad at you?"

"Everything, that's what," she said solemnly. "He kidnapped Mrs. Knox, that's the lady what owns this house. He's got her stuck in a dungeon someplace, prob'ly." She shrugged and wiped her mouth with her pajama sleeve. "Or she's in the quarry. That's where Robert's gang hides the dead bodies."

He opened up the "Uncle Wiggly" game and laid out the board and pieces. He didn't know quite what to say. Caitlin had her mind made up that Robert was some kind of monster. After a moment he said, "Want to go first?" They played a few minutes, Caitlin absentmindedly having taken two turns in a row; and he shook the dice, determined he wasn't going to say anything to encourage her over-lively imagination. "Six." He moved his piece along the board. "Sometimes we get crazy ideas about people we're not sure we like very much."

Caitlin shook the dice and moved her piece. "Five! I'm gonna win." Unfortunately, she landed on "lost in the woods" and had to go back three. Eyeing Jake's piece, two spaces back and gaining fast, she reached for a red card. "Great! I get another turn."

Giving her a serious look he said quietly, "Do you know what I'm talking about, Caitlin?"

Ignoring the board directions to "go back three," she headed for Dr. Possum's house and a sure win. "Of course. Robert's mean and tells lies all the time. Aunt Margaret doesn't believe me, but I know I'm right. He stinks."

"Granted, you don't like him. But why would he kill Mrs. Knox?"

"Because he wanted her money." She sniffled once or twice, then sneezed violently.

He handed her a tissue. "Robert has plenty of money. He doesn't need Mrs. Knox's. Here, mop your nose." She grimaced, but did as she was told. Jake said quietly, "You just resent your stepfather for some reason."

Caitlin paid no attention to this silly remark. She tossed the tissue on the floor. "He tells lies all the time. He puts worms in Mom's medicine so she throws up. And he never called the doctor for her. I know because I saw him pretend to dial, only he didn't." Moving her piece to Dr. Possum's, she beamed. "I won!"

Jake folded up the game board, not sure he'd done the right thing, getting Caitlin to talk about her feelings of resentment toward Robert. She hadn't changed her mind. He hadn't made any headway at all.

Margaret said from the doorway, "The doctor can see you if we go down right away, so get up and put some clothes on, Caitlin. Want me to give you a hand?"

Caitlin glowered. "Is he gonna give me a shot? I'm 'llergic to shots."

"Not that I know of." Margaret sighed tiredly. "Come on, get up and get dressed."

Jake followed Margaret out into the hall. She closed the door and put her fingers to her lips. "Shh, I don't want her to hear. Look what I found under her pillow. Caitlin's sure it's full of worms or bugs, put there by Robert to make Sandy sick."

Jake turned the pill over in his palm. "Robert gets all kinds of samples in his work for that drug firm. He's always in and out of hospitals and doctors' offices." He frowned at Margaret. "Maybe he thought he'd...help Sandy on his own."

She gave an unhappy shrug. "God, I don't know what's going on. Take a look at what else I found." She showed him the snapshot and earring. "Mrs. Knox, that's who the woman in this picture has to be...she's wearing these earrings, the same as the one you found in Robert's car."

Jake's face was expressionless, but the line of his mouth tightened as he compared the earring in his palm with the wedding snapshot. There was a heavy beat of silence.

"I...I don't understand all this. The lies—" Margaret began. "Why didn't he tell anyone he'd been married? The entire time *we* were engaged, he never said a word about having been married to your sister. And he let me—and I'm sure Sandy, too—believe he had no money. You said your sister had a trust fund he inherited when she died. Yet we used to talk about scraping up money to buy a house someday." She swallowed hard.

Jake frowned. "It was a nice amount of money. Hardly something you'd forget."

"He could have made bad investments, been unlucky," Margaret speculated.

"That's a possible explanation, but—"

"Oh my God!" Margaret felt chilled all over.

There was something in her tone of voice that Jake didn't like. "What?"

"Sandy inherited Great-Aunt Caitlin's estate just after they got married. A lot of money." Sarcastically Margaret said, "He doesn't have to worry about charge accounts now."

"I remember you telling me he doesn't have any credit cards—" Jake fished a folded slip of paper out of his wallet. "You're wrong. He charged four tires for the Fiat less than a year ago. I found the charge slip in the glove compartment. See?" He held out the paper.

She looked at it, then stared dumbly at the signature on the bottom. "My God, *she* paid for four new tires!"

"What are you talking about?" Jake snatched the sales slip and scanned the signature on the bottom in disbelief. "I didn't even bother to look at who signed it. I just assumed it was Robert." He gave a low whistle under his breath. "Polly Knox's name is turning up everywhere. Something's going on here."

"I don't understand any of it," Margaret said bitterly. "Robert's got all these secrets...his marriage to your sister, money he's inherited, this affair with Mrs. Knox—" She glared at Jake, daring him to contradict her. "It was an affair. He was her lover and lied about never having seen her before renting this house. Now he's married to Sandy, and Caitlin swears he's giving her pills to make her sick." She shivered, feeling a terrible sense of apprehension. "I'm afraid."

Jake gave a grim sigh. Then he had a thought. "Ask the doctor what the pill really is when you take Caitlin down to see him. If he says the pill's harmless...we've laid one ugly suspicion to rest."

"COME BACK in half an hour." Margaret dropped a quick kiss on Jake's mouth and climbed out of the car. She extricated a still-complaining Caitlin from the back seat and went into the doctor's office. Jake drove two blocks up the street and parked in front of a combination toy, gift shop. Okay, half an hour, he thought, checking his watch. Time enough to pick up something to make Caitlin feel better.

The bell over the door jangled as he entered the shop. He noticed a woman behind the counter, then looked again. It was the same woman who'd stopped by the house last night. Violet Chadwick. "Hello, we met last night," he said politely.

She arched an eyebrow. "Oh, yes, you're . . ."

"Jake McCall. I was at Mrs. Knox's house last evening."

She smiled briefly. "Can I help you with something?" Her tone was bored, as if she had little time to waste.

He looked around. "I was hoping to find a good game or book for a little girl." The shelves were stacked with all kinds of things. He picked up a Parcheesi game and glanced at the rules on the back. Pretty straightforward. Maybe too simple. Caitlin was one hell of a complicated kid. After more thought, he chose a few books and took both the game and books to the counter. "I'll take these." Smiling, he added, "Nice shop. You must get a lot of business."

She rang up the sale and put the merchandise in a bag without bothering to look up. "We do all right."

He took out his wallet. "Do you work here full-time?"

"No," she muttered. "Only part-time, to keep busy." Her narrowed eyes flicked over him. "Are you a friend of the people renting Polly Knox's house, the Schuylers?"

"Actually, I'm Robert Schuyler's former brother-in-law. He was married to my sister a few years ago."

There was a small silence, then she said hurriedly, "Did you want to include a card? I'm sorry, I should have asked if you wanted this gift wrapped."

"Maybe I'll get a card, but never mind the gift wrap. It'd be off in two seconds." He took his time selecting a card from a nearby rack. "Vermont's lovely. Do you know if they have any hiking trails, waterfalls, that sort of thing?"

"I can't help you. I've only been here a short time. I'm from Connecticut."

He glanced up. "Really? I spent a few years in Connecticut. My sister and brother-in-law owned a house in Fairfield. Ever been to Fairfield?"

"No," she said icily, handing him the change. She banged the register drawer shut.

Shrugging, Jake picked up his package and left the shop. He found a phone booth and made a few business calls, then went back to the doctor's office and parked. Margaret and Caitlin were just coming out. He leaned over and opened the door. "Great timing."

"Yes," she agreed, turning to make sure Caitlin had fastened her seat belt. Jake gave Caitlin the package.

"For you. A get-well present."

"Wow! Thanks! Can I open it, can I?" Caitlin already had the books out of the bag and was tearing the lid off the Parcheesi game.

She seemed much better, almost her old feisty self. But Margaret looked decidedly worried. She glanced at Caitlin, then said quietly to Jake, "She's got the flu, some bug going around town. The doctor says she'll be better in a day or two." Looking quickly into the back seat again, she said, "I asked him about Sandy, and he said he'd only seen her once, that she looked run-down. He prescribed rest and vitamins. I mentioned her nausea—I thought Caitlin might have caught the flu from Sandy—well, he said he and Sandy talked about her vomiting, and in his opinion it was a touch of food poisoning." Margaret swallowed hard. "Jake, I don't know what's going on. He had no idea Sandy had gone to Florida. Why did Robert say the doctor had suggested she take a Florida vacation?"

Jake started up the car and pulled away from the curb. After a moment he reached over and gripped her hand, hard. "Good question, and one I don't know the answer to... like a good many things about Robert. They don't add up."

Margaret drew a deep breath. "There's more. The doctor said he hadn't heard from Sandy since the first visit. He expected her to call back, and she never did. When I asked if she should finish the antibiotics he'd prescribed for her, he didn't know what I was talking about. He'd never prescribed anything for her. So why was that pill in the bedside table?"

Caitlin unsnapped her seat belt and leaned over the front seat. "I know why. Robert put it there, after he put bugs in it to make Mom throw up."

Jake gave Margaret a sideways look. "Did you show him the pill?"

She nodded. "He said it was a barbiturate. There was a code number on it. He said you couldn't mistake it for anything else."

"It could be Robert's, left there accidentally, or something Mrs. Knox left behind. It's her house.

Sandy might even have found it in the medicine cabinet and meant to throw it out.

"I might believe that if there wasn't something else that was extremely disturbing. Finding the wedding snapshot and the pill took over my thoughts for a while, and I forgot to tell you about something." She paused for a breath. "My Great-Aunt Caitlin—who died and left Sandy her estate—hired a nurse for several months before she passed away. I found the nursing contract—actually, Caitlin found it—in a box in the attic with some of Great-Aunt Caitlin's old clothes. Sandy must have stored it up there. Well, the nurse was Polly Knox—only she was Polly Merrill then."

Jake's mouth hardened. "What are you saying? That Polly could have known about the will and that a niece was the heir?" He stopped abruptly. The reality of where his thoughts were leading him was just taking hold. "If Robert discovered from Polly that your aunt was leaving money to one of her nieces he could have originally thought that you were to get the money—and set up your first encounter at Killington where you were skiing."

"I was mentioned in the will. But she changed her bequeaths constantly. It was kind of a game with her. She told me once when I was ten that she'd cut me out of the will if I didn't clean my plate. We were visiting for the weekend, and she fed us lima beans. I couldn't stand them," Margaret said quietly.

"Ugh! I hate lima beans. They make me sick," Caitlin remarked from the back seat.

"Your theory sounds very scary," Margaret went on in a trembling voice. "He could have broken off the engagement when he found out Sandy was the heir, not me. Polly must have gotten another look at the will. Or maybe the will was altered one last time, and Polly didn't discover it until it was too late. Robert had already met me, and we'd gotten engaged.''

He gave her a long look, knowing deep inside that this was true. ''We need solid proof. And so far all we have is speculation. The earring and Polly Knox's signature on a charge receipt is not enough.''

She stared at him. ''How do we get more proof, one way or another?''

Jake drew in a ragged breath. ''There's only one thing we can do now to make sure Robert isn't trying to kill . . . Sandy.'' He raked his hand through his hair and said, ''I know we haven't mentioned murder out loud, but that's the only conclusion we can come to at this point. And the only way I can think of to get some proof that Robert goes after women with money—and then tries to kill them—is to pay a visit to my sister's doctor in Connecticut.'' Margaret squeezed his hand, telling him that she understood how hard this was for him. ''If we find out there was anything remotely suspicious about Betsy's death . . . I'll ask to have the body exhumed . . . then find Robert and kill him.''

Margaret, in a strained and low voice, said, ''Sandy will have to be told when she calls next.''

''If she calls,'' Jake said softly, wrapping his arms around Margaret.

AN HOUR LATER they were on their way to Connecticut. Mrs. Till—over Caitlin's strenuously voiced objections—came to the house to baby-sit.

The drive down to Fairfield was tense. Margaret's mind was full of worry and fear. She was half dreading what Betsy's physician might say.

Jake stopped at a gas station near Hartford to call and make sure Dr. Wellstone could see them. By two-thirty they turned off the Interstate onto a local highway. It took them another fifteen minutes to reach the doctor's office.

He was a thin, wiry man, half-balding, and his eyes were bright blue and shrewd. He had a slight limp when he walked. He gave them both a discerning look as they sat down. "I have only fifteen minutes to spare," he said apologetically. "I know you've driven a long way." He raised an eyebrow. "What did you want to know?"

Jake leaned forward in his chair. "Was there anything at all suspicious about Betsy's death? I'll get straight to the point, could she have been…murdered? By some untraceable poison or an injection of air?"

Dr. Wellstone hesitated, then said, "No, her heart gave out. Yes, it was unexpected, but she had a heart murmur."

"She'd had it all her life. You told her the medication was taking care of it, that she didn't have to worry."

Dr. Wellstone picked up a pen and rolled it between his fingers. "True, and under ordinary circumstances, she shouldn't have died." His face grew somber. "Unfortunately she was that one in a million that medical science can't predict."

Jake shook his head. "You didn't perform an autopsy—how can you be sure her death was due to her heart murmur?"

Dr. Wellstone pursed his lips, then put the pen down on his desk blotter. "We didn't perform an autopsy because, frankly, her husband denied us permission. I would have liked to pin down the cause of death more exactly, but with her heart and the asthma attack she suffered that night, well, it didn't seem... necessary. Her husband was with her when she died. He described what happened and called for a nurse immediately. However, it was too late. She was gone."

"All you have is her husband's word about what happened that night." Jake gestured with a despairing hand. "So you really don't know."

"I won't waste your time or mine, arguing. Your sister had a serious medical condition—"

"Which was controlled successfully for years," Jake interrupted grimly.

The buzzer on the desk sounded twice. Jake rose. "Thanks for your time, Dr. Wellstone. It was most informative."

They were both grimly silent on the drive back to Vermont. Jake's face was rigid and flushed with suppressed anger. Margaret was still too stunned to say much. She sat, her hands clenched in her lap. *Naive* was not the word to describe how ignorant she had been about Robert. She'd fallen for his easy charm, flattery... How could she have been so easily deceived?

As for poor Betsy's death—if it had been murder, Margaret had to admit it had been ingenious. She'd died in the hospital, with the best of medical care available, surrounded by doctors and nurses. Then Robert had played the grieving widower—and had sat back and inherited all that lovely money.

Chapter Ten

Luckily there was little traffic on the road by the time they turned off Route 100 onto North Hollow Road. They'd stopped in Rochester to buy cough syrup and markers for Caitlin, who no doubt would still be awake. It was a little after nine o'clock, with the air sweet smelling and fresh from so much rain. Jake squinted as a pair of headlights flashed in the rear-view mirror. Margaret twisted in the seat and took a look. "Someone else on the way home."

"He's not in much of a hurry." Jake glanced in the mirror again and shifted to second. "He could have passed us back there."

The road rose ahead in a series of looping curves, but visibility was good because of the moon and the lack of fog. Jake turned the wheel right. Loose gravel rattled beneath the wheels. "Do you think Sandy's called tonight?" He tried to keep concern out of his voice. Margaret had enough to worry about.

She pushed her hair back tiredly. "I don't know. God knows what I'm going to tell her—" She stopped speaking abruptly as a wash of backlight flooded the car. Coming closer and closer, the car following had turned on its brights.

"Damn." Jake squinted and flipped the mirror up. Absently he checked that his seat belt was fastened. "Got your seat belt on?" Margaret nodded and he went on grimly, "It gets narrower and steeper around the next curve."

Margaret took another quick look out the back window.

"All we need is a jerk tailgating." He tightened his hands on the wheel. The road surface was poor, mostly ruts with patches of thin, hard, finely ground stone toward the crown of the road. He had to ease up on the accelerator for a right curve because he felt the rear end of the car drifting. "Hang on, I don't like this."

Margaret put a hand on the dashboard, bracing herself. She could feel the rear end vibrating as the car slewed sideways toward the black pine trees, spectral against the background of bare rock and earth.

"No place to pull over and let him pass," Jake muttered. "We'll just have to put up with him until we get to the farm."

Suddenly the headlights grew huge in the rearview mirror, and their car was hit from behind, causing it to skate sideways with no control, bouncing off the rusted fencing that edged the shoulder of the road. "My God," Margaret gasped.

Jake threw a furious look in the mirror. The headlights came up again, blinding him, the gap between the cars narrowing to nothing, and he thought of the pivoting tendency of the car's rear end if they got hit again; then the car would automatically go into a skid.

There was an explosive pop as the car's brake lights broke. The car lurched suddenly sideways, and immediately its mass began to dominate its momentum. The fence loomed, grew gigantic in the windshield, then was gone as the car skidded away.

"Hang on!" Jake was trying to control the wheel instinctively now. Left to right the car skidded, wider to the left and again wider to the right. He knew better than to jam on the brakes. He smelled the clutch burning, and the car went into a slow spin. One part of his mind was thinking of how he would wring the neck of the drunk in the other car if they lived long enough for him to get his hands on him; and another part heard the brittle bumping of their tires across the ruts as the car spun in a series of crazy loops, the headlights from behind appearing and reappearing in the windshield. He thought he heard Margaret scream, then they were rammed again, obliquely this time, just behind his door handle. He braked, but it was no good, they were going too fast. The car went straight through the fence with barely any impact. He felt the drag of his seat belt and a moment of weightlessness before the car tilted nosedown and struck something—a boulder, a series of saplings—and struck again, rolling, tumbling, now on its side, now on its roof; and the long sound of raw metal scraping against stone as it slid to a stop. Their speed, momentum, died; the silence was eerie; the moon reflected oddly in the cracked mirror.

"Are you all right?" He grabbed Margaret's shoulders. Her eyes were closed. A streak of blood ran down her cheek. He shook her gently. "Margaret, we've got to get out!'' She stirred; her dazed eyes cleared as they focused on his face.

"My God, what happened?"

He was already unsnapping his seat belt and hers. He pulled her out, stumbling, rolling as they landed. Then he got to his feet and scooped her up in his arms. He looked for the nearest cover, and limped behind a pine tree.

There was a noise, an eerie crackling, and red light glowed all around. The explosion made the ground shake and the trunk of the pine tree tremble against his shoulder. A second explosion rocked the car. The air reeked with the smell of burning gasoline.

His coat had been ripped at the shoulder; he swallowed hard. The shock of the crash was just setting in. The car hadn't met much resistance as it had hit that fence; it had broken away like so much wet paper. Numbly, he held Margaret in his arms and watched the car burn.

"I can stand," she mumbled.

"Sure?" She nodded, and he set her on her feet, keeping a firm arm around her waist. He was just realizing the "accident" had been deliberate. Not a drunk out for a few laughs, recklessly forcing someone off the road. No, they'd been the target of an attempted murder. Nothing showed from the road above. No light, no dim face, no sign of anyone leaning through the gap in the fencing to make sure there were no survivors.

"Can you walk?" He brushed the tumbled hair away from her face. In the fading glow of the fire her face looked pale.

"I'm okay, just shaken up some," she whispered.

"We'd better get moving. Head for the house. It's not that far. We can make it." His breathing was painful, it felt suspiciously like a cracked rib; and a warm wetness was dripping down his hand. "Come on." A light wind sprang up as they climbed back up to the road, and when he glanced down the mountainside, he saw sparks blowing from the burned-out shell of the car. The smell of burning rubber was thick and acrid in his nostrils, coming stronger now.

They limped onward. The woods were silent and peaceful, moonlight sifting through the trees to dapple the road. Yet Jake was aware all the time of a mounting tension. Danger. The word was so clear in his mind, it might have been written in fiery letters against the trees. Whoever had forced them off the road might return.

Ten minutes later they stumbled up the front steps of the farm. When they went inside, Mrs. Till drew a shocked breath. "Land sakes, what happened?"

"We had an accident with the car," Margaret told her. She gave a little laugh. "Believe me, it's a long walk up the mountain." She sank down in a kitchen chair. "Where's Caitlin?"

"She's in bed. I fed her supper. Never mind her." Mrs. Till wiped her hands on her apron. "Let me get you a cup of tea. You both look like you could use it."

Margaret shook her head. "No, you go along home. We'll be fine." Mrs. Till looked skeptical, but listened and left.

The back door closed behind her, and Jake took off his coat, awkwardly easing it past his shoulders. He winced. "God, I'm tired. I could use a drink, and I don't mean tea." He headed slowly to the living room and the whiskey decanter. Margaret pushed him gently onto the settee. "You're in worse shape than I am. I'll get you a drink." She poured it with shaking hands, and he gulped it down. A fire was burning in the fireplace. A log shifted, and a shaft of sparks curled upward.

Jake leaned back and closed his eyes. When he opened them again, she was kneeling in front of him, dabbing at his bleeding left hand with a towel. There was a bowl of pinkish water on the table, a pile of gauze bandages and a pair of scissors.

"I'm glad to see you're conscious again. How do you feel?"

He said slowly, "Like someone who's supposed to be dead at the foot of the mountain. I don't know how you can move."

She grinned. "Women are the stronger sex, didn't you know that?"

"Someone tried damn hard to kill us...." His voice trailed off, and he pounded his fist on his knee. "If this is tied in together with Robert...I'll kill him with my bare hands."

"We can go to the police, tell them everything and have an all-points bulletin put out for him." She got up and went over to the phone on the hall table.

He raked his hair back with his good hand. "Nothing will stand up in court. He'll sue for false arrest, raise hell . . . and see to it Sandy meets the same fate as Betsy. An unfortunate accident, brake failure on her car, a fall downstairs. She's in love with him, she'll believe whatever he tells her until it's too late."

"What about Polly Knox? If she's in this with him, when she comes back from Europe the police can question her, maybe she'll break and tell the truth."

He looked at her out of ice-cold eyes. "What if she doesn't come back? What if she's dead?"

Margaret drew in a long breath and stared at him, speechless. Just then there was the dull thud of something falling upstairs. "Caitlin," she said, frowning. "I'll check on her."

Caitlin was examining the contents of her shoebox and looked up guiltily as Margaret came in. She allowed her face to be wiped with a damp washcloth. Margaret's eyes were drawn irresistibly to the shoebox as she straightened the pillows and put a jumble of dominoes back in their box.

"Those things in the shoebox, where did you find them all?" she asked casually.

Caitlin's jaw dropped comically; for once she seemed to be at a loss for words.

"I found it the other night when you had that nightmare. It fell on the floor and I picked up the things that fell out," Margaret went on chattily. "What about that picture of Robert?"

Caitlin shrugged. "I found most of the stuff in the den, but the picture was in the sewing room, under a drawer. He looks dumb in a mustache. How come he said he'd never been in this house before he and Mom rented it? That's the front porch and the big maple tree in the picture. I reco'nize the woodpecker hole in it."

"Never mind about that now," Margaret said evenly. "Where in the den did you find the other things?"

"On the shelf, behind the big red dictionary."

Margaret drew a deep breath and thought hard. Had Polly Knox hidden Robert's picture and other things as evidence? Maybe she was afraid of him, and the snapshot was a crude form of life insurance. She'd cleared off to Europe in one hell of a hurry. What if Caitlin was right and Polly was dead—hadn't Jake just said the same thing, that she'd never gotten to Europe? What if her body had been weighted and thrown in the quarry. Such a handy place for dead bodies....

"I was coloring and then I decided to look for something to read and dropped my crayon behind the books. I was trying to get my crayon out, and there was all this stuff behind the dictionary." Caitlin's face radiated blameless innocence.

Margaret stared at the shoebox. The letter. Maybe that was the evidence they needed to convince the police. "What about the letter? Was it behind the dictionary, too?"

Caitlin nodded. "Yeah, do you want to read it? It's all about fights over money." She dragged the cover off the shoebox and rummaged inside. Handing the letter to Margaret, she added, "See? He signed it 'love,' too."

Margaret scanned the letter quickly.

Dear Polly, everything's going well. I've rented an apartment in Allston, too expensive, but it's suitable for my needs. About the money, call it a loan—with the big payoff down the road. Trust me, that's all I ask. Let's face it, I'm no saint. You of all people ought to know that. But it's what we agreed on. We're a team, and a good one. Don't mess things up now. And honey, if we're talking threats, I can make plenty of my own. Your hands aren't clean. In the meantime, think over what I said. I'm going to Killington on Wednesday. Plan to call you when I get back.

Love, R

Margaret couldn't move. She stared numbly at the letter in her hand, seeing only a blur of white and black. After a moment she drew a long breath and checked the end of the letter again. "It doesn't have Robert's signature on it. It's just signed *R*."

"Yeah, I know. But it's his letter," Caitlin said with a wide yawn. "He always signs notes for Mom like that, with an *R?*"

"But it could be someone else's letter." Margaret looked at Caitlin who yawned again and shook her untidy head.

"Nope. It's gotta be his."

Margaret rose and picked up the shoebox. "I'd like to show this to Jake, the little wooden box, too."

"Sure." Caitlin hunted around among the toys and games and handed over the wooden box. "Just 'member to push the squares backward, every other one. Or it won't open."

Margaret went downstairs to find Jake standing in the front hall. Their eyes met as she came down the last step. Shadows lurked in his. She gestured toward the kitchen. "I've got something to show you. A letter Caitlin found. It's from Robert, at least I think it is. And it's written to Polly Knox. Let's sit down and go over the clues Caitlin's collected. Then we can decide if it's enough proof."

A few minutes later they'd spread everything out on the kitchen table. The earring, the wedding snapshot, Robert's picture on the front porch, the letter. Reading it quickly, Jake said grimly, "There's nothing damning about it on the surface." He drew a harsh breath. "Robert wrote it. I'm sure of it."

Margaret paused in the act of opening the wooden box. "All right, let's just say it's his. Robert had an apartment in Allston. And the letter mentions Killington. Of course that's where Robert met me, on that ski trail."

She was pressing the squares of an inlaid wooden box. As it opened, he asked, "What's that?"

"Some of Great-Aunt Caitlin's bills and papers stored up in the attic. Nothing important, a maintenance agreement for her TV." Margaret went through the papers, one by one. "Another for a VCR, and the contract with Polly Merrill."

Jake's gray-blue eyes darkened. "If we can get Polly to testify against Robert—if she's really in Europe and not dead—we could get him. Call the local travel agency and see if she booked a flight to Europe."

"What about the car? Shouldn't we report the accident first?" Her green eyes were huge and exhausted looking.

He shrugged. "First let's figure out if Polly really went to Europe. The car can wait. It's not going anywhere." He rubbed his aching side and read the letter again while Margaret called the travel agency.

"There's no booking in Polly Knox's name for Europe," Margaret said when she came back. Her voice shook. "Oh, Jake, what are we going to do?"

"We find Robert and Sandy. Where were they staying in Florida?"

"The Surfside Motel, near Orlando. But they've moved on by now. Sandy said they would drive around and stop when they felt like it."

He was silent for several seconds. "Is there a travel guide in the house? The oil companies sell them, with motel listings."

She nodded in relief. "In the den. Sandy looked through it before they left. I don't think they took it with them."

As she found the travel guide and ran her finger down the first page of listings, she said, "This seems so useless. Couldn't we notify the Florida police?

"What do we tell them? There's a possibility Robert killed my sister and is going to murder yours?"

She bit her lip. "It all ties in. Polly was my Great-Aunt Caitlin's nurse and found out what was in her will. She must have told Robert I was the niece who was inheriting everything. Then my aunt changed the will. When Polly found out it was too late. He was already engaged to me and had to break off our relationship to court Sandy."

Jake shook his head. "The police would never believe us. I don't know if our accident tonight is tied in somehow—but it's a damned odd coincidence." He gave a bitter laugh. "Robert probably knows people who'll kill for the price of a drink."

Margaret, shaken, sank down in a chair. "I don't believe this is happening." She was pale; lines of strain showed around her curving mouth.

"Look at this from the point of view of the police. You're the bitterly jealous sister. You lost the man you were in love with, and maybe you wanted to get your hands on her money, too. They might even suspect you if anything happened to Sandy."

"That's crazy," she said dully. "Anyone who knows me..."

He shrugged. "You have two strong motives for murder—jealousy and greed." He gave a mirthless smile. "I'd make the short list, too. Especially after they got through talking to Dr. Wellstone and learned I'd been asking questions, trying to prove Betsy'd been murdered. Presumably I'd be bitter because I hadn't inherited my sister's money."

"But we know Robert's a killer. He was with Betsy when she died—there was no autopsy."

"We *suspect* Robert's a killer, but we're a long way from proving it. All we have are a few pieces of circumstantial evidence. We've got one option now. To get to Florida and convince Sandy she could be married to a cold-blooded killer."

Chapter Eleven

Or Sandy could already be dead, a small voice in the back of Margaret's mind whispered. Fear and anger knotted her stomach, blocking out all thoughts of anything else. Margaret stared at the pages of the travel guide, trying to concentrate. Suddenly she remembered that picture of palm trees on the right-hand page. The motel with two pools.

"Jake, I remember Sandy marking a motel in Lakeland."

"Let's check the location." He spread a large map of Florida out on the table. "If they headed south, they had two choices, the east coast or the west coast. The Everglades rules out anything else."

She let out a silent breath. "Unless he had plans for her that included the Everglades." Miles of saw grass, mangrove swamp and alligators. "For all we know he's already killed her." Her eyes filled with tears.

"Stop it," he said sharply, turning toward her and taking her into his arms. "Margaret," he said softly. His arms were sliding around her waist, holding her close.

There was a noise from the hallway, the unmistakable shuffle of seven-year-old slippered feet. Margaret sighed and turned her head.

Caitlin was standing there with her bathrobe buttoned up all wrong. She had a battered teddy bear under her arm. "I woke up. I had to go to the bathroom." She frowned darkly. "There's no more toilet paper. I called, but you didn't answer."

Margaret went over and put her arm around Caitlin's shoulders. "Okay, go back upstairs. I'll get more toilet paper from the linen closet."

Caitlin's eyes narrowed as she stared at Jake. "Wow! There's blood on your shirt, and it's all torn!"

"And you've got a cold and shouldn't be out of bed," Margaret told her, gently but firmly. "Back to bed."

"But I'm thirsty. I need another..."

"I'll get you a drink," Margaret promised, bending to drop a kiss on Caitlin's rumpled head. "Upstairs now." Deftly, she began walking her upstairs.

Jake's voice floated after them. "I'll just call and report the accident. Better late than never. The police—"

Oh no, Margaret thought wearily. That's all they needed, the magic words: *accident, police.* Sure enough...

Caitlin halted dead in her tracks. They'd made it as far as the landing. "What accident? Is someone else dead?"

"No, Jake's car ran off the road. He's reporting the accident, that's all. Come on, I'll tuck you in." She managed to get Caitlin back in bed, a lengthy process because everything had to be just so.

The window had to be opened another half inch, the vaporizer refilled. And then Caitlin still hadn't gone to the bathroom.

Margaret shook her head and went to refill the toilet paper holder, and after Caitlin came out of the bathroom, it took another ten minutes to settle her in bed. "Good night, honey." Margaret leaned down and gave her a hug and kiss.

Caitlin frowned. "Where are my magic markers? You promised you'd get them for me."

The markers were burned to a cinder at the foot of the mountain, Margaret thought grimly. As they both might have been.

"We'll have to get more tomorrow." She sat down on the side of the bed and took Caitlin's hand. "I've been thinking."

"What?" Caitlin asked suspiciously.

"Well, Jake and I are probably flying to Florida tomorrow. I was going to ask Mrs. Till if she could stay with you for a few days, but I remember she said she was off to Canada day after tomorrow. Which leaves us with a large problem." Margaret drew a breath. "The problem is, who's going to baby-sit you while I'm gone? Your father's in Europe someplace. I can't reach him, and anyway—" She took another breath. "Things are complicated, to say the least."

Caitlin's face set into a mutinous frown. "I wanna come, too. I wanna go to Disneyworld."

"But you're not feeling well," Margaret said, feeling Caitlin's forehead with the back of her hand. "Hmm, your fever's gone."

Magically Caitlin's face beamed with hope. "See, I'm better, and there's nobody to baby-sit." She sighed happily. "So I get to go to Florida, too."

Margaret hesitated, then gave up. "I guess so." Squeezing the small hand in hers. "I'm worried about your mom...and Robert. There might be something...wrong."

Caitlin nodded. "I told you there was. Robert's *mean.* Ackshully, he's a mean old pig, and I hate him." She yawned widely, "But everything's gonna be okay because Madame Zorina says I'm gonna save everyone."

"I hope she's right." Margaret got up and turned out the bedside lamp. "Sleep tight, honey. Sweet dreams."

"'Course she's right. Madame Zorina's magic." Caitlin yawned again and wriggled down under the blankets. "G'night."

When she descended the stairs, Margaret found Jake waiting at the foot. "You look all in," he said, concern in his eyes.

"I am," she agreed, half-laughing. "I can hardly keep up with Caitlin. She's got more energy than a herd of wild horses."

"Then I'll tuck you into bed, and call and get reservations on a flight to Florida tomorrow morning." He slid his arm around her shoulders and walked her back upstairs.

Halting at the top, she looked up into his eyes. "We have to take Caitlin with us. She's feeling better, and Mrs. Till's away. There's no one to leave her with."

"Okay, we'll manage somehow," he said with a wry smile.

With reluctance she crawled into bed and pulled the covers up. She yawned as his arms encircled her body and he laid a gentle kiss on her lips. "Go to sleep. I'll be up in a few minutes." Deftly his fingers unbuttoned her blouse and slipped it off. Her bra followed, then her jeans. He slipped a nightgown over her tired head and tucked her in again. "I'll be back soon."

Those were the last words she heard, and in a few moments she was sound asleep.

In the morning she dragged herself out of bed and took a hot shower, hoping it would bring her back to life. Jake was already downstairs making breakfast, judging from the aroma of coffee and toast wafting up the stairs. She grabbed a salmon wool dress, pumps, stockings, and got dressed. After winding her hair into a neat chignon, she applied lipstick and blusher in a vain attempt to bring color into her pale face and blinked at herself in the mirror. The reality of everything flooded back to her tired mind.

They had to find Robert before he added Sandy to his list of victims.

As she got downstairs the phone was ringing, and she picked it up. It was Violet Chadwick, calling to ask if they'd heard anything from Polly Knox. She said chattily, "By the way, I heard there was a terrible accident up on North Hollow last night. A car burned. The police said it was totalled. You don't happen to know whose car it was?"

Margaret leaned against the doorjamb. "The car belonged to my friend, Jake McCall, and by some miracle we walked away from that accident."

"My, my, how lucky," Violet said worriedly.

"Yes, now about Polly Knox, I haven't heard anything. As a matter of fact, I'll be gone myself for a few days. I'm flying to Florida sometime today."

"Oh, I see—well, I won't keep you," Violet said briskly. "Have a pleasant trip." She hung up with a sharp click.

Margaret sighed and replaced the receiver. Turning, she saw Jake coming from the kitchen. He was scanning the front page of the morning paper.

"They're holding an inquest into Vern Boyce's death next week," he said quietly. At her startled intake of breath, he shook his head. "Don't worry. I talked to the police last night. They know we're going to Florida. That's all cleared. They'd like you to be around for the inquest. As things look now, they're leaning toward accidental death. They found several places on the quarry wall where he hit before entering the water—if he was drunk and fell in."

TWO HOURS LATER they were in the departure lounge at Montpelier Airport, in front of Gate 5 to Orlando, via Boston. Jake was sitting beside Margaret, his thigh just brushing her knee. Her salmon wool skirt was crushed between them. Through the folds of wool she could feel the hard, warm touch of his muscular leg.

Caitlin was sitting on the other side of Margaret, peeling the paper from a stick of grape bubble gum. Popping it into her mouth, she chomped happily.

Margaret reached up and felt her hair with her fingertips. It was sticky. Bubble gum. They'd spent the better part of the last hour on the drive to the airport listening to Caitlin read excerpts from her notebook.... "Robert's a rat, but we're gonna get there just in time to save Mom. Madame Zorina says so. Robert's gonna go straight to jail, and we can all go to Disneyworld." Leaning her folded arms across the back of the front seat so that her nose was right next to Margaret, Caitlin had blown a big bubble, which burst all over Margaret's hair. What a mess!

Margaret got to her feet. "I'm going to the ladies' lounge to try and clean the gum out of my hair! I'll be right back."

Caitlin jumped to her feet. "I have to go to the bathroom, too. And I'm thirsty. Can I get a soda?"

"No, we don't have time. Maybe on the plane," Margaret said as they walked past the gift shop display. The store was full of jugs of maple syrup, books on Vermont, handmade wool afghans, wintry ski posters. Her mind drifted to Jake and herself in a cozy ski lodge, the firelight flickering in a stone fireplace. No, in bed would be even better. Tangled limbs, his warm skin sliding over hers. . . .

"That lady over there keeps staring at us, really hard," Caitlin said idly in between bubbles.

In spite of herself, Margaret paused and looked around. There was no one in sight but a couple of teenagers, a pair of black-robed nuns, and a thin man in a very ugly bow tie. "Come on, we don't have much time," she said shortly, marching on toward the ladies' lounge.

Caitlin hurried to keep up, looking over her shoulder. "Well, she's not there now, but I saw her and she was looking at us, she really was." Caitlin sounded disappointed.

Margaret shouldered open the lounge door. "Oh, come on, it was just some woman watching people pass by. She was probably bored and had nothing better to do.''

Caitlin stalked past her indignantly. "I saw her. And she wasn't bored, she was *staring*." She disappeared into the toilet stall and the lock clicked. Margaret walked over to the sink and fumbled in her purse for a comb.

"I notice things like that," Caitlin said from behind the partition. "'Cause when I grow up I'm gonna be a writer. You know, I already told you that."

Inwardly, Margaret heaved a sigh. She tugged the comb through her matted, gummy hair without much success.

"I'm collecting information for a book."

"On what?" Margaret muttered, probing a sore spot on her scalp. Maybe a pair of nail scissors would cut off the worst of the gum.

"It's on murder," Caitlin said happily. The toilet flushed, the door opened, and she came out. "Seeing as I'm practically an eyewitness, sort of."

Margaret shoved the comb back in her purse and swallowed hard. "Let's sincerely hope not."

"What? Oh, yeah, well...I know Mom's gonna be okay, but there's always Mrs. Knox and Vern Boyce." She leaned closer and said in a clear, carrying voice, "It had to be Robert or someone helping him. *An accomplice!*"

And from the far side of the partition came the sound of a flushing toilet, a door opening, footsteps...Margaret turned and glanced quickly at the woman leaving.

It was one of the nuns, and she was eyeing Caitlin with a sort of dreadful fascination. Margaret forced a brief smile as the nun gave her a wintry stare and washed and dried her hands in utter silence.

Caitlin lodged her gum in the corner of her cheek and turned on the water. She soaped her hands. "There's all kinds of evidence. Like Robert didn't get rid of Mrs. Knox's clothes after he kidnapped and killed her. And he left the boat in the quarry. There's the letter and his picture. I wonder if he tortured her first."

Margaret, quite familiar with torture by now, closed her eyes and said wearily, "That's very interesting."

"Sure, he could have cut off her—"

Opening her eyes, Margaret said, "Not one more word!" The nun shook her head in grim disbelief and left.

THEIR FLIGHT LANDED in Orlando about four o'clock. Although it was getting late, the sun was hot and the sky was still a brilliant blue with dollops of ice-cream clouds piled on the horizon.

Margaret stood with Jake at the baggage carousel. The claims area was crammed wall-to-wall with milling people, half of whom were looking for luggage, the other half looking for friends and relatives.

It was a madhouse. She found a vacant chair and sat down tiredly. Caitlin was standing next to a nearby pillar, examining the crowd. Looking for the mysterious woman she'd seen in the airport departure lounge in Montpelier. Caitlin was certain the lady had boarded the plane, and Margaret hadn't been able to convince her the poor woman deserved privacy on her trip to Florida.

Jake piled the bags at Margaret's feet. "Look, I'll give the Surfside Motel in Orlando a call and see if they know where your sister and Robert went. They might have called ahead and made reservations at the next motel."

Blowing a bubble, Caitlin sauntered over. "Let's go to Disneyworld first, because what if they close it down or go on strike and I don't get to go?"

"No, we find your mom and Robert first, then we go to Disneyworld," Margaret told her firmly.

"Phooey." Caitlin sighed and looked around, then grabbed Margaret's shoulder. "I saw her! She's over there, on the other side of the baggage thing. She's right next to the old lady with the black hat." She shook Margaret again. "Aren't you coming with me? We can catch her."

"No," Margaret said flatly. "Leave the poor woman in peace."

Caitlin gave her a look of belligerent contempt. "Great! That's just great. She could be part of Robert's gang, his *accomplice!* She could be planning to kidnap me for all you care!"

Margaret suppressed an impulse to laugh out loud at the thought of a gang member capable of such stupidity. "There isn't any gang. It's just some woman going on vacation."

Jake came back from the phone and car-rental booths. "Ready to go? Come on." He helped her up with one large hand, somehow grabbing Caitlin and their bags, propelling them toward the terminal exit.

It was ninety degrees outside and humid. The warm air struck Margaret's face like a blow, rising from the pavement in stupefying waves. They walked through the parking lot toward the car Jake had rented, a silver-blue Buick Regal.

He bent to unlock the trunk and stow away their bags. Margaret leaned against the front passenger door and tried not to breathe. Her wool skirt was sticking to the backs of her legs.

Caitlin came skipping around the front of the car. "There's something dead between the cars in the next row. I think it's a cat, only it's so squashed you can't tell." Her eyes were round with innocence.

"Oh, God," Margaret said tiredly. "Caitlin, please."

"It prob'ly got runned over. There's a lot of blood. And flies. Flies are crawling all over it."

She felt she was going to throw up. And wouldn't Caitlin love that, she reminded herself. Resolutely, Margaret choked back the remains of the in-flight meal.

Caitlin was saying, "All that blood. The car must have got spattered with it. What if it was Robert's? All we have to do is look for a car with blood all over it."

"Get in the car and be quiet." Margaret yanked open the back door.

But Caitlin still had her pièce de résistance to offer. "It looked like the head came off."

"Enough, young lady," Jake said quietly. "If you open your mouth again, I'll turn you over my knee and whale the living daylights out of you."

That did the trick. Caitlin gave him a reproachful look and climbed in the back seat.

Jake slammed the trunk closed, and they got in and drove off toward the highway. "The Surfside desk clerk said he heard Sandy mention Lakeland as their destination. So we'll head down there," Jake said as he pulled onto the highway. "It's quite a drive. Once we get to Lakeland we'll register at a motel, and I'll see if I can get a line on where they went."

Margaret sighed and leaned her head back on the neck rest. After a moment she put on a pair of sunglasses against the late-afternoon glare and stared out at the shimmering heat rising from the road. She closed her eyes and dozed fitfully. She woke with a sense of panic when the motion of the car stopped.

Jake was looking down at her with a smile. "Wake up, sleepyhead. We're here at the motel."

She sat up and took off the sunglasses. The sun was setting. She rolled down the window and breathed deeply. The sky was blazing red and gold, and there was an ocean breeze to take the edge off the oppressive heat.

Jake got out of the car and stretched, and she flipped down the visor mirror and stared at her reflection. Her mouth was pale, and there were shadows beneath her green eyes. Haunted by Robert? Or by her growing fear that they might not be in time to save Sandy?

They went inside the motel to register. Jake gave her a wry look. "A double and a single?"

"Right," she murmured sweetly.

She dragged a loudly protesting Caitlin away from the soda machine. The coin return was broken, and she'd been playing it like a one-armed bandit and winning. Margaret made her return almost two dollars in nickels and quarters to the desk clerk.

The moment they got to their rooms, Caitlin switched on the TV, found cartoons and turned up the volume loud enough to make the walls shake. Then she sauntered to the bathroom and shut the door.

Margaret marched over and turned off the TV, bumping into Jake who was putting their bags on the bureau. His hands came out and caught her arms, and she found herself held tight to his body. Startled, she looked up into his face. He wore an expression of frustration and lingering desire.

Her body was pressed close to his, her heart racing, her breasts crushed against his jacket. He was very tall, looming over her. There was no room to move, but a single step backward and she bumped into the double bed.

His hands tightened on her arms, and her lips parted. It was a moment lost in time, they might have been alone in the world with a thousand things to say—all about love and passion.

He drew a deep breath, and suddenly his eyes were laughing down into hers. "Guess my timing leaves something to be desired."

She never had a chance to reply because the toilet flushed, water ran in the bathroom sink and the door opened, all in a matter of seconds.

Caitlin came out of the bathroom and looked suspiciously from Margaret's flushed face to Jake's tall, broad back. They were now the width of the bed apart, but she must have had eyes in the back of her head. "Dumb, drippy love stuff," she said disgustedly.

MARGARET WOKE REFRESHED the next morning and got out of bed. She went over to the window and pulled back the curtains, letting in the clear, golden morning light. Her eyes flickered to the palm trees dotting the edge of the parking lot. No sign of a breeze.

It was sunny and hot, just like yesterday. She'd better hurry and dress. Jake had said he wanted to be on the road by nine. It was almost half past eight. Maybe she ought to wake Caitlin. She gazed across the room at the humped blankets on the other bed.

No, she would let her sleep awhile longer. Jake had said he would make a few phone calls this morning and try to track down reservations Sandy and Robert might have made with the large motel chains.

She walked past Caitlin's bed and into the bathroom where she washed her face with bitingly cold water. She felt frustrated, caught in a dangerous spiral from which any activity was better than doing nothing.

She found a road map of Florida in the desk drawer, along with colorful brochures of assorted tourist attractions. She fanned them out on the desktop. Hmm, there seemed to be an inordinate number of alligator farms.

Sighing, she turned to the map. Lakeland. That's where they were now. Tracing her finger along the black line past Disneyworld west from Orlando, she found Lakeland. But where, she wondered helplessly, was Sandy?

"I'm hungry." Caitlin's voice, neglected sounding, startled Margaret. Then the sound of something breaking made her wince. Caitlin had knocked an ashtray off the bedside table as she'd yawned and sat up.

Margaret picked up the pieces. "Give me time to shower and dress and we'll find Jake and go eat." Dumping the glass in the wastebasket, she ignored Caitlin's brooding look of indignation and went into the bathroom.

When she came out and slipped into her clothes and picked up her purse, ready to take Caitlin next door to Jake's room, all the little girl had to say was, "I was ready ages ago. They'll probably be out of pancakes, and that's all I feel like having."

"Good, you're both up." Jake grinned as he came out of his room. "I made more phone calls. No luck with most of the big chains. They must be staying in smaller motels."

Margaret stared at him, unable to block out the thought of Sandy being found dead in a motel bed, Robert the innocent, grief-stricken husband.

"What's the matter?" Caitlin tugged at her hand. "You look real unhappy."

She managed a small smile. "Oh, nothing. Just thinking about your mom."

"Don't worry about Mom. Everything's gonna be okay." Caitlin's voice held determination and unshakable faith in herself and the predictions of Madame Zorina.

"That's right. We'll find Sandy and straighten this out," Jake said, putting his arm around Margaret. He squeezed her shoulder gently. "Okay now?"

She reached up and touched his hand. Then she sighed and said quietly, "Okay."

They went down to the restaurant where Caitlin ate a royal breakfast of pancakes, sausages, fresh orange juice and milk. Margaret picked at her order of toast and scrambled eggs, not really tasting anything. She couldn't help wondering why Jake was so quiet. Every once in a while she caught a glimpse of something in his eyes. Was it worry? He didn't want to frighten Caitlin, of course.

She drew a deep breath, trying to relax. Caitlin looked at her across the table. She wore a milky mustache. "I forgot to bring my Barbie dolls."

"Well, you brought other books and toys," Margaret said encouragingly.

"I could have taken Barbie swimming," Caitlin mumbled through a mouthful of sausage. "She likes swimming. So do I."

Margaret shot a quick glance at Jake. "What do you think? Have we time to let her swim for a half hour or so?"

Pushing back his jacket sleeve, he checked his wristwatch. "If you make it quick. Take her back to the room and change while I settle the bill here." He shrugged. "We'll try and make up time later once we get on the road."

Ten minutes later Caitlin was jumping into the azure waters of the swimming pool. And Margaret sat on a lounger, thinking about Sandy and where she was and if she was all right.

Suddenly Caitlin was standing, dripping on the cement pool surround. "Aren't you going in?"

"No, we don't have time."

"Oh, well I'm kinda cold." Caitlin shivered and hugged the thick towel around herself. Margaret rubbed her back and legs with the towel ends, trying to warm her up.

"There, that better?"

Caitlin's freckled face glowed up at her in the sunshine. "Uh-huh, I had fun."

Giving her a quick hug, Margaret picked up her clutter of shoes and shirts, and they trailed back to the motel room. Caitlin peeled off her bathing suit and climbed into shorts and a cotton T-shirt while Margaret packed everything into their suitcases.

"Can I go out in the hall? I think I dropped one of my toys." Caitlin was hopping up and down by the half-open door.

Margaret frowned thoughtfully, and hesitated, then said, "All right, but don't go far. I'm almost packed." Even as she spoke she realized she was talking to the air. Caitlin was gone.

Chapter Twelve

Out in the hall Caitlin looked first in one direction, then the other, frowning. She hadn't been fooled, not one bit. Robert's gang had obviously followed them here to Florida. Prob'ly the gang was working in pairs. The woman in the airport terminal had boarded the same plane. She'd been sort of dumb, staring like that. Easy for a master detective to spot. The other one, though. Hmm, maybe the other gang member had been the old lady in the black hat.

Sure. Some really bad guy, bent over and wearing a gray wig. He was prob'ly reporting back to Robert right now, telling him where they were, and that Caitlin had been swimming. Robert wouldn't even believe that she could swim. He always made cracks about how kids got in the way and should keep quiet. Once he'd even said he would cut her tongue off if she stuck it out at him again.

Caitlin hadn't told anyone about that.

The master detective frowned. Anyway, she wasn't scared of old Robert. He was just a big jerk.

She decided to go left, up the wide metal stairs to the second floor. There might be a telephone that the old lady in the black hat would use to call Robert.

Carefully she dropped a small cloth doll near the foot of the stairs, in case Aunt Margaret checked to see if there really was a lost toy. Suddenly, down below, a door slammed. A man came out and walked away, carrying a brown suitcase. Caitlin shrank back into the shadows on the stairs. The cement walls closed in on her. Her heart thudded like drumbeats in a horror movie.

Nothing moved. Nothing stirred. The master detective had escaped detection. Slowly she relaxed. She waited another few seconds, then climbed the remaining stairs to the second floor. It was darker up here. Shadowy corridors stretched off to the left and right. Inky blackness painted the distant end of the hallway. The cloak of darkness beyond the last door was impenetrable. Did light from the overhead fixture seem bright from down there? Could she be seen?

She moved quickly to the left, sliding her body against the wall. A burst of muted sound came from behind the nearest door. A TV. Whoever occupied that room prob'ly wouldn't be opening the door.

The master detective reached in her pocket for a piece of bubble gum. She unwrapped it and took a large bite, chewing slowly, watching the nearest door with suspicion. More noise, clapping and laughter. It sounded like a game show.

She blew a big bubble, popped it and licked it off her cheek, her shrewd glance taking in something else of interest down the hall. A large, gray metal machine in a lighted niche. Every once in a while it made a whirring noise, then a muted kind of a clunk. Clearly this needed further investigation.

She strolled up to it and lifted the lid. Lots of sparkly ice cubes winked up at her. More than anyone would ever need, she thought, idly blowing another bubble.

As she watched, another load of ice cubes fell into the bin from some mechanism in the back. It had little red knobs on the side, and funny dials. She leaned over the edge of the bin and fiddled with the knobs, turning one, then another, wondering what would happen. She twisted one knob too hard.

A whole lot more ice cubes began gushing forth into the bin, making a terrible racket. The knob came off in Caitlin's hand as she jumped back in surprise. There was a loud explosion, and thick, oily smoke curled up from the bottom of the ice machine.

MARGARET CLOSED the suitcase and snapped it tight. One last look around to make sure she had everything.

Suddenly someone knocked on the door. The motel desk clerk was in the hallway with Caitlin by the hand—as if she were some exotic species of chimpanzee. Caitlin was scowling. The desk clerk handed her over and said, "She was running around unattended."

"Thank you, my niece was just looking for a toy she dropped." Margaret was uncomfortably aware of a guilty gleam lurking in Caitlin's eyes.

He shrugged. "She did a job on the ice machine up on the second floor. Damned thing can't be fixed until tomorrow. The manager said he'd appreciate it if you kept the kid under control for the rest of your stay.''

Caitlin said loudly, ''I didn't do anything. I was just watching it make ice. I wanted to see how it worked.''

She came inside, and Margaret closed the door and gave her a long look. ''Why did you go upstairs to the second floor?''

Caitlin gave her a perfectly innocent stare. ''I was looking for my toy, like I told you. See, I found it.'' She held up a small cloth doll.

A doll Margaret had never seen her play with before. She gave her another long look and said, ''I see.''

For some reason Caitlin seemed somewhat subdued as they went out to the car and helped Jake load the suitcases. She climbed in back and got out her notebook and pencil.

Jake got in front beside Margaret and closed his door. He looked over at her. ''I found the motel they stayed in two nights ago. They didn't say where they were going, but the desk clerk said Sandy looked well enough. They went out to dinner, then came back early. Robert told the desk clerk Sandy tired easily. They spent the day sailing.''

She drew a breath of relief. ''That sounds innocent. I mean, maybe we're jumping to conclusions. Maybe there isn't anything to this whole mess—''

He shrugged and pulled the car out onto the highway. ''There's one way to find out. We confront Robert, see what he says.''

They drove past a shopping center. Across the street a bank sign flashed the temperature. Eighty-nine degrees at 10:47. A typical sweltering Florida day.

She glanced at Jake, wondering why he hadn't turned on the air-conditioning. He grimaced and said, "One little problem with the car. I noticed it yesterday, just as we got to the motel. The air conditioner's on the fritz, so we'll have to suffer for the day."

"I'm hot," Caitlin remarked grumpily from the back seat.

"Too bad," Margaret told her. "We're all hot. You're not the only one."

"Yeah, but all I have is a dinky little window. The front seat has two big windows," she complained, scribbling away in her notebook. In a matter of minutes she'd started some sort of list, humming, a look of dreamy contentment on her face.

Margaret sighed and flipped the visor down against the glare of the sun. She wondered how long it would take to find Robert and Sandy.

Jake leaned over and gripped her hand reassuringly. "Come on, don't think what you're thinking. We'll get there, I promise."

She flashed him a wan smile. "Thanks, I was just wondering how many places we have to check."

"I covered most of the motels at this end of Route 75. If we hit the ones on Route 17 and head for Marcos Island, we should find them. There won't be any more places to look except the Everglades."

And that was one place they didn't even want to think about.

The wind came through the open windows like armloads of hot, dusty grit. The highway stretched to the horizon. Nothing but palm trees, traffic and hot scorching sun. Margaret's skin was moist with perspiration, the dust sticking to it like glue.

Predictably, Caitlin began clamoring for a bag of donuts as they stopped at a gas station to fill the tank. The breakfast had proved to be less than filling.

Margaret looked questioningly at Jake who sighed and gave in. If they were lucky, the donuts would keep her busy for a whole ten minutes. Jake paid for the gas and drove to a nearby donut shop and went inside. When he came out and got back into the car, they jounced out onto the highway again.

Caitlin ate three donut holes and declared there was nothing to see. "I'm not having any fun. This is boring." Her mouth crammed full, she said, "After we find Mom, I'm going to Disneyworld. You promised, right?"

"That's right," Margaret agreed.

"And I'm gonna meet Mickey and Donald."

"Right."

"And go on all the rides as many times as I want."

"Okay," Margaret sighed. Jake shifted in the seat and gave her a sidelong look, and she saw the pained laughter in his blue eyes.

"Heaven help us," he muttered under his breath.

Another half hour or so later they passed two more shopping malls and several motels. Jake and Margaret took turns going into the motels, asking the clerk on duty if they'd had a Mr. and Mrs. Robert Schuyler registered in the past day or two. They had no luck.

They passed another shopping mall, crowded with cars glittering in the sun-drenched air. And a Mc-Donald's restaurant, which Caitlin spotted.

"I need a hamburger and large fries. Besides, I have to go to the bathroom."

It was only twelve-thirty, and they could get out to stretch their legs. Jake turned in, found a parking space, and they went inside.

The lunch crowd was just building, and the air-conditioning must have been broken. It was hotter inside than it was out in the sun. The counter girls sagged over the shining metal counter. "Take your order, sir?"

Jake got ice tea with extra ice for himself and Margaret, and a hamburger, large fries and a milkshake for Caitlin. Margaret tugged on his shirt. "Get catsup for Caitlin's fries. She won't eat them without it."

He looked around and frowned. "Do you want to eat in here? It's hotter than the hinges of hell."

"No," Margaret said, pushing back her damp hair. "The idea of eating anything makes me feel sick, anyway, but the heat in here is unbelievable."

Caitlin returned from the bathroom, and Jake paid for their food. Pushing open the glass door as they went outside was almost a physical shock. Stupefying heat rose off the asphalt.

They got back in the car and Caitlin munched on the hamburger contents separately.

Jake drove slowly around the back of the restaurant to the exit lane, and Caitlin reached over the front seats to turn on the radio. It came on full blast, all but deafening. Margaret grimaced and groped for the volume control numbly and lowered it. Caitlin flopped back into her seat and became totally engrossed in squeezing catsup on her fries.

"Fasten your seat belt," Margaret reminded her, glancing into the back seat. The catsup spurted out of the little plastic pack in Caitlin's hands, dribbling all over the large fries.

She leaned back in the front seat and closed her eyes. The hours passed, and they drove on under the hot sun, stopping at each motel they saw, asking in vain about Mr. and Mrs. Robert Schuyler. Finally it was almost seven. The sun was setting, a glowing ball of orange in the growing dusk. Caitlin was cranky, hot, tired and hungry. They were all exhausted. Clearly, they had to stop for the night.

"Okay, next motel we see," Jake promised. The glittering red neon sign up ahead announced Vacancy. Jake pulled in and parked, and they all went in to register. Caitlin was yawning widely, but declared she was really thirsty. Could she have a soda?

Margaret nodded tiredly and groped in her purse for change. Handing her more than enough, she turned to sign the register as Jake collected their keys and picked up the bags.

They trailed wearily up to their rooms, Caitlin sucking noisily on her drink. Margaret wondered with the half of her tired brain that still functioned, if Caitlin was ingesting too much junk food and caffeine.

Jake unlocked her door and put their bags inside. "Give me time to take a quick shower, then we'll go down to dinner."

She nodded and pushed Caitlin inside, kicking off her shoes. Lord, she was tired. She sighed and told Caitlin to sit on the bed and watch TV for a few minutes. "I'm going to take a shower. I'll be out in a minute."

Caitlin yawned and flopped on the bed, already lost in some car chase on TV. Margaret unzipped her dress and went into the bathroom. She turned on the water and stepped in the tub, letting the cool water run in streams over her exhausted body.

Just as she'd toweled off and pulled a cotton dress over her bra and panties, Caitlin let out an ear-splitting scream. For a wild second her stomach dropped and she didn't know what had happened.

Caitlin was still yelling, and she ran into the bedroom.

"There's someone at the window!" Caitlin's face was white with fright. "A big face with staring eyes. Like a skull! Or a ghost!"

Margaret ran to the window and pulled the curtain shut, completely closing out the growing dark of night. "For heaven's sake, there wasn't anyone. It was your imagination."

"Oh, yes there was. I saw him, or her. I don't know if it was a man or a woman out there, but I saw something out there." Caitlin swallowed hard, shivering with dread. Even master detectives felt fear once in a while. She remembered noises she'd heard outside, just before she'd seen the face. Scraping sounds. No flesh-and-blood person could be out there. It had to be a ghost.

But why would ghosts be following them around, she reminded herself. No, it was Robert's gang. It had to be. Vaguely she wondered how he'd managed to get ghosts to join his gang.

"You saw your own reflection out there." Margaret pulled the curtain to one side and looked out.

There was no one in sight, only the silvery glow of the full moon.

Caitlin glared at her. "I know I saw someone. And we didn't have the light on, either. The moon's out and it's full, just like Madame Zorina said it would be. Danger! We've got to be real careful!"

Margaret ran an exasperated hand through her hair. "Never mind that full moon nonsense. What were you up to at the window?"

"I thought I saw some funny lights," Caitlin said reasonably. "Like a UFO landing. It circled, so I shined my flashlight up at it. I was signaling." She was wearing her best innocent look.

"Where did you get the flashlight?" Which Margaret now saw lying on the floor by the window where Caitlin had dropped it.

"I found it."

"Where?" she said grimly.

"In the lobby while you were getting our room key. I found it by the soda machine, and I thought it would be a good idea if we had one. We might get a hurricane and the electricity could go off. They get hurricanes in Florida all the time," Caitlin said confidingly.

She wasn't sure how to approach this bit of information so she ignored it, turning slowly around and picking up her purse. Just then Jake banged on the door. "Margaret, what's the matter? Let me in. I heard Caitlin yelling."

She opened the door. "Caitlin thought she saw something at the window and screamed. It was only her imagination."

"No, it wasn't. It was a ghost," Caitlin muttered stubbornly.

Margaret sighed and exchanged wry glances with Jake who ruffled the top of Caitlin's head with a large hand. "Nighttime can be scary when you're in a strange place."

"I wasn't scared. Or only a little," Caitlin admitted in a small voice.

"Well, you don't have to be scared," Margaret told her, hugging her tight. "We're here, and we wouldn't let anything happen to you. No matter what."

ENTERING THE RESTAURANT and sitting down to a relaxing meal was wonderful to Margaret. So... normal... soothing, shutting out threatening possibilities like people staring in windows and cold-blooded murder.

Caitlin ordered fried chicken, cole slaw and French fries. Margaret looked determinedly out the window while she dribbled catsup on her fries in long, scarlet ribbons.

Jake suggested they have onion soup, and it came in a small brown bowl with French bread and melted cheese on top. It tasted wonderful.

"Can I have another order of fries?" Caitlin looked at Margaret hopefully. Catsup dripped down the front of her T-shirt like a modern painting done by the splash and splatter method.

"No," Margaret said firmly. "How about a salad?"

"Or dessert? How about an ice-cream sundae?" Jake suggested, getting out the menu again. After some thought, Caitlin ordered a strawberry sundae, and Margaret drank a cup of tea, feeling herself slowly unwind inside.

Jake paid the bill and they left the restaurant. They walked along the narrow flagstone path that circled around behind the motel.

It was dark now. Only the rising moon and the lights from the motel rooms cutting bright coins on the surface of the pool. Everything was deathly still. A few birds twittered, then fell silent and began again almost as if they were watching them stroll along the path.

Margaret decided she wanted to buy a paper. She touched Jake's arm. "Would you take Caitlin back to the room for me? I want to run back and pick up a newspaper. There might be something in it Sandy and Robert would notice. I don't know—an advertisement or tourist attraction. Motel listings, anyway." She handed the key to her room to Jake.

"Don't be long. Caitlin's going to teach me how to play Old Maid. I think I'll need help."

Margaret reached up and kissed the strong line of his jaw. "Five minutes, no longer. Bye."

Exactly seven minutes later she was hurrying along the flagstone path, the evening paper under her arm. Overhead the full moon was riding high over the inky lace of the treetops. She passed alongside the pool. The night wind was picking up. Margaret shivered a little. Across the pool a whispering rustle of branches. Just the wind rustling in the bushes, she thought, staring across the rippling water of the pool. She stood there a second, feeling her heartbeats thud against her side. Silence weighted the air.

Shaking her head, she walked on, hastening her steps. There was no warning. Only a sharp blow against her back, and the flagstones tilted, the palm trees angled, everything was suddenly sliding sideways until the lights on the horizon were vertical and she was falling through the air. Weightless. Slow motion. She was falling headfirst into the pool with someone's arm locked around her neck, one hand savagely across her mouth to keep her from crying out.

The shock of hitting the water momentarily drove the breath from her lungs. Down, down, and she was desperately kicking, clawing her attacker, trying to fight free.

But she was tired, all but exhausted. Her lungs dragged for air and found none, only water.

The attacker was murderously determined.

Her fingers scrabbled blindly at the arm tight across her neck, feeling the soft flesh. Kicking out with her feet, she pushed off from the bottom of the pool, and they lifted, rising, shooting upward through the blue-white world into the air.

The hand covering her mouth slipped free, and she took a breath, heaving air deep into her lungs, and they filled, giving her strength and life. Her lungs, her entire body was suddenly bursting with rage.

She continued struggling, closer now to the pool's edge. Her attacker must have been using the coping at the top for leverage, clawing at her face, her hair, yanking her backward and under the water once more.

Rolling over on top of her, holding her head under, her attacker's legs were twined tightly around her body—like snakes. Holding her down. Her vision was darkening and the last throbbing of life and eternal night was coming.

She let herself go limp, sagging motionless, no longer resisting the force of the arm hooked across her windpipe, the body locked against hers like a lover, slowly windmilling in a dance of death.

Don't move. Don't think.

The pool was darkening, going black. God, she felt cold. To survive she had to move, to fight. But she had no strength to move. Her lungs felt as if they were bursting. She couldn't feel her hands or feet anymore. *This must be what it's like to die.* And oh, God, she'd had a warning. Caitlin had mentioned the full moon. Madame Zorina had told her to be careful around water.

From a great distance she heard voices, laughter, and slowly, carefully, she felt the pressure ease from her windpipe, and she was floating facedown in the water.

She felt numb, nerveless and oh, so sleepy, but knew this feeling was a trap. She had to resist the growing dark, the death-bringing black of night. It was so close, so close now....

She kicked feebly and turned her head to the right. Yes, there was the coping. It seemed so far away, but when she reached out a hand, there it was. She'd reached the edge of the pool.

She clawed and hooked her fingers on the coping, rolling sideways, lifting her head clear of the water. And then breath eased back into her lungs. She gasped for air, gagging and coughing. The pain in her lungs was scalding, like a balled fist driving into her chest.

The voices grew louder now, voices changing, no longer conversational, but yelling, shouting. She couldn't understand what they were saying.

Hands reached down and hauled her out of the water, rolling her over. Life-giving hands pushing in and out on her ribcage.

She realized someone was on his knees, giving her artificial respiration. And somewhere in the back of her exhausted mind came the thought of poor, drowned Vern Boyce. This was what it had been like for him, only he hadn't come back from the dark world of death.

She kept coughing, and vomited rapidly, ignominiously.

"What happened?" the desk clerk asked, handing her a towel. "My God, lady, you almost drowned!"

People were standing, staring down at her, shaking their heads, talking in low voices.

She wiped her face and streaming eyes. God, she felt weak. The damn towel kept sliding out of her nerveless fingers. And she was shuddering uncontrollably. In a whisper worse than a scream she gasped, "Someone pushed me in. Someone was trying to kill me."

The desk clerk helped her to a lounger and covered her with a blanket. He didn't appear to have heard what she'd said. "Look, we'll get you a doctor. Make sure you're all right."

She didn't have the energy to fight with him, she barely had the strength left to wipe her face again with the edge of the blanket.

He chewed nervously on his mustache. "It's motel policy when a thing like this happens, lady. Oh, here comes the doc now."

The doctor was a rather corpulent, sad-looking man with a black bag. He looked into her eyes, down her throat and ears, took her pulse, listened to her lungs and questioned her persistently. Had she had a few drinks with dinner?

"Someone pushed me in and held me under," she said, her voice hoarse and shaking. She pulled the blanket around her. "Someone was trying to kill me."

The doctor gave her a lightning glance and frowned at the desk clerk who shrugged and said it was the first he'd heard of that. The tone of his voice suggested it was a figment of her imagination.

She looked steadily into the doctor's eyes and said, "I didn't have anything to drink. I was going back to my room after dinner, and someone pushed me into the pool and tried to drown me."

His eyes narrowed. "Do you know who it was?"

"No," she admitted helplessly. "I never saw his face."

"You never got a look at this guy's face . . . the person you say pushed you?" By this time the desk clerk wasn't bothering to hide his disbelief.

"No." Her denials seemed to drift away on the night air like smoke—as nebulous as her attacker seemed to be.

"Look, Ms. uh . . ."

"Webster," she supplied tiredly.

"Look, Ms. Webster." He handed her a cup of coffee. "We, that is the management, don't want any trouble. You didn't see who pushed you. You've got no real proof, nothing except your story. I'm not saying you're wrong, only . . . maybe you're mistaken. It was dark, right? And you were hurrying. You could have lost your footing, slipped and fallen in. Maybe you hit your head on the cement coping. Know what, lady? You should be counting your lucky stars and maybe lay off the booze, not run around making wild accusations about someone attacking you.''

She looked up at the desk clerk, stunned. How could he be so damned casual about attempted murder? Anger washed over her, leaving her shaky.

If there was one thing she knew, it was that someone had tried to kill her and come damn close. She sipped the coffee, forcing the hot liquid past her bruised throat. It hurt like hell to swallow.

The desk clerk turned to the doctor. ''Wouldn't it be better if she went to a hospital?'' He meant better for the motel. Attempted murder was bad for business.

The doctor shrugged and put the stethoscope in his black bag. ''It might be better if she were admitted. She's suffered a severe shock.'' He snapped the bag shut. ''But it's her decision. I can't force her to go.''

They were talking about her almost as if she wasn't there. As if she was an object to be disposed of any way they wished.

She huddled in the damp blanket and stared at the azure water in the swimming pool. It was peaceful, calm and empty—except for the newspaper floating on top of the water. And her shoes bobbing hideously up and down. Her purse must have gone straight to the bottom.

For one terrible moment time ceased, and she was feeling that nauseating blackness, struggling, kicking and clawing; and she knew she was going to die.

She shuddered and turned her head. She couldn't look at the pool. The bright moonlight mocked her. Why hadn't she taken Madame Zorina's warning seriously? Why hadn't she been more careful?

The next few minutes passed in a blur. The desk clerk got the pool scoop and retrieved her shoes and purse. He dumped the sodden newspaper in the trash and put the shoes and purse on the flagstones by her chair. They lay in a puddle at her feet, the water spreading, darkening the stones.

She couldn't seem to stop shaking. Some huge source of physical energy was jerking at her exhausted joints. She spilled the coffee and had to carefully put the cup down on the flagstones by her purse.

It's fear, she thought. Fear was making her shudder and shake. Why on earth had she gone back to buy the paper? She straightened up with difficulty.

"I'm not going to a hospital," she said firmly. "I'm going back to my room."

The mob of curious onlookers was melting away. She wondered exactly how she was going to crawl back to her room. She didn't think she could get to her feet, pick up her belongings and walk that far without falling flat on her face. Especially since there was something very wrong with the way her legs were acting. Her knees were shaking. Crawling, prickling fear was sweeping over her flesh in horrible constant waves.

Chapter Thirteen

Jake, with Caitlin at his heels, pushed past the desk clerk and doctor, took one look at Margaret and said, "My God, what happened?"

"I fell in the pool." She struggled to her feet with Jake's help, knowing it would be wrong to show fear in front of Caitlin. She had to remain cool and calm. She filled her lungs with a shuddering heave, throwing all her energy into control. She managed a weak smile and said, "Come on, let's go back to the room."

Jake picked up her things and they left, Caitlin trotting silently alongside. As soon as they got to the room and the door was shut behind them, Caitlin said, "How'd you fall in? It was Robert's gang, right? Prob'ly the old lady in a black hat. Did she hit you with her cane?"

Jake turned on the TV and told Caitlin to sit down and watch it, then he pushed Margaret toward the bathroom. The wet blanket dropped to the floor as he took her in his arms and held her tight. Kissing her hair, rubbing her back, he whispered hoarsely, "Thank God you're all right. Everything's going to be all right now. You're safe with me." He rocked her tenderly, his arms folding her close.

His face blurred before her eyes. "Someone pushed me, tried to kill me. Oh, Jake, he held my head under. I thought I was going to die." Tears ran down her cheeks, and her hands clutched at his shirt. "I couldn't breathe. I was so scared. I don't know why he let go, maybe people were coming. I thought I heard people talking, then suddenly, he was gone."

Her knees gave out then, and she sagged against him. Her head burrowed into his warm chest, and she sobbed—great heaving sobs of fright and thankfulness.

With a half-muttered curse, he tightened his arms around her, buried his face in her hair and pressed her closer. "I don't know what the hell's going on, but...thank God you're okay. Shush, oh, honey, shhh," he whispered between soft kisses.

Caitlin's raised voice came through the door. "If it was an accident, how come people were saying you thought someone pushed you in? Was it because the moon was full? Madame Zorina said—gosh, I'd better write all this down in my notebook!"

The large hand rubbing Margaret's back went quite still. He drew a deep breath and said quietly, "Do we call the police?"

As quietly as he'd spoken, Caitlin had heard him. "Yeah, we should call the police. I could tell them Madame Zorina said you were in danger when the moon was full, and I could tell them it was that woman following us, or the old lady in the black hat. They're both members of Robert's gang! I could tell them I saw her!" She seemed to think this was indisputable evidence.

Margaret took a sobbing, hiccuping breath and said between sniffles, "What do I tell them? Someone pushed my head under and held it there? No, I didn't get a glimpse of his face, and oh, yes, I'd been warned by a fortune-teller to be careful around water while the moon's full? If they take down my statement, which is doubtful after they hear the nonsense Caitlin's spouting, they'll laugh their heads off and tell me to quit drinking."

Jake rubbed her back, caressing her gently. He whispered soft words of endearment and encouragement. With each one Margaret felt his strength and tenderness working a healing. She clung to him, feeling herself slowly emerging from the hell of life-threatening fear. The warmth of his body thawed her wet, half-frozen body. Then he tipped her head up and kissed her, and the last of her anguish dissipated like a frost in the summer sunlight. She felt light-headed, encircled by love. Shaping her hands to his face, she gave herself up to his kiss. "Oh, Jake, I love you," she whispered against his mouth.

"I know, I love you, too," he murmured hoarsely. "I'm not going to let you out of my sight until this mess is over." Kissing her again, he pushed her gently toward the shower. "Get out of those wet things. I'll bring in your nightgown and put Caitlin to bed."

She nodded and wiped her wet face with the back of her hand. He gave her a smile of encouragement and left, the door closing with a soft click. She took a hot shower, dried herself off, got into the nightgown Jake put by the sink and climbed into bed.

He got in beside her, leaned over and turned off the light. "I'm staying here with you. Don't tell me no. Just go to sleep." He drew her into his arms, cradling her against him, and she held on with no intention of ever letting go.

"I'm sorry," she whispered. "I never should have gone back for the paper."

"Hush, don't be silly." With one arm supporting her head, he gently smoothed damp tendrils of hair from her cheeks. "Just go to sleep. Things will look better in the morning."

But would they? Somehow she didn't think so. And long after Jake's breathing had become measured and soft with sleep, she lay beside him, gripping the blankets tightly up around her neck.

Her life before the pool incident seemed cloudy, almost surreal. The only reality was that she'd almost died about... she took her arm from beneath the blanket, checked the time on her wristwatch, and saw with grim amusement that it had stopped.

Right now, safe within Jake's arms, she was less frightened than she'd been. Not that the situation was really any better. Her mysterious attacker was still out there somewhere. He could easily try again. It was just that fear seemed unable to stay at the same pitch for very long.

She was safe with Jake beside her. But inside she knew cold, sickening fear remained coiled like a snake, ready to strike her at any moment. But if she could haul herself beyond the shaking horrors, keep the fear lying down the way it was now, maybe she could come up with some constructive thinking.

She lay in Jake's arms, trying not to tremble. And then she thought—what if Caitlin was right and some woman had been following them all this time? Even an old woman with a black hat. That arm around her neck could have been a woman's. But no, the maniacal strength of the attacker's arm had been that of a man.

After a while tears filled her eyes, blotting out the darkened motel room.

MARGARET LAY quietly, huddled in Jake's arms, dreaming. It was starting again, the sickening blow between her shoulder blades, and she was falling. Then her lungs were filling with water, aching. The whole world was blue water, dizzying, endless death.

The murderous arm tightened around her neck, choking off her air supply. In the final seconds she fought, clawing, kicking, but it was too late. Everything was fading, going pitch-black. Everywhere there was nothing but water and the awful gasping pain. She was dying.

She woke all at once, gasping for air, sitting straight up in bed. Her throat was raw with pain, her breathing coming in panicky shallow breaths.

It was almost dawn. Outside it was cool and misty. The sun hadn't had time to bake off the dampness from the night before, and the air was actually breathable. The sun rose, a dazzling gold in a cloudless blue sky.

The pale morning light striking through the curtains shouldn't have struck her with such dread. She struggled awake, caught in the half panic of the dream. She felt infinitely vulnerable. Her horrifying dream had vanished, but reality was far worse.

A tremor shot through her body, and Jake sat up and took her in his arms, holding her tight. "Come on, honey. It's okay, I'm here. I've got you."

She held on to him, light-headed, almost weak with relief. "It seemed so real. Oh, Jake, it was horrible, I was scared to death!"

Crushing her against his chest, he vowed, "No one's ever going to hurt you again. Never." There was a faint catch in his low voice. She nodded, and he gave her a bone-crushing squeeze. "That's my girl."

But her mind was a blur of questions. What if her attacker came back? And most of all—why would someone try and kill her?

With an effort, she took a deep breath and managed a small smile up at Jake. "I'm okay now."

They got up, showered and dressed, and got Caitlin up for breakfast. In the restaurant they sat by the window at a small round table. Margaret drank coffee and tried to act as if she wasn't sitting in a shimmer of fatigue and fear. Jake kept Caitlin busy with a cheery conversation about dolphins and other Florida sea life.

He only had half her attention. Margaret could see Caitlin's brain whirling, sifting through last night's pool incident. She waited, braced for Caitlin to launch into a discussion of Madame Zorina's warning.

"So that's why we have to be careful about pollution and what we dump in the sea. Other creatures live there," Jake explained.

Caitlin nodded and worked her way broodingly through fresh orange juice, scrambled egg and toast with curls of butter. She paused to give Margaret a gimlet-eyed stare.

Was she frightened? Margaret wondered. That was the last thing they wanted, but lying about things wouldn't help. Margaret gave Jake a warning look over Caitlin's head then said quietly, "What's wrong? You're awfully quiet."

A large blob of egg fell off Caitlin's fork and she tidily brushed it off the tablecloth onto the floor. "I'm kinda worried about Mom. Maybe the person who pushed you is gone. What if it was the old lady from the plane and she's gone to meet Robert? Do you think she killed Vern Boyce, too? And besides, how am I gonna save everybody if we're stuck here?" Her voice was a penetrating hiss.

Jake reached over and put his arm around her. "Right after you finish that milk, we're leaving. We're going to find your mom and Robert and everything's going to be fine. I called half the motels in the state, tracking them down. They took the highway we're on now. Finding them is just a matter of time."

But did they have enough time, Margaret wondered.

They finished breakfast, went back to the room, packed and were on the road west, along the route Robert and Sandy had taken, by nine-thirty.

By eleven, Caitlin was hungry again, and they stopped to get her something to eat. This kept her relatively quiet, except for the slurp of soda.

But just after they'd passed through a major highway interchange, Caitlin became abruptly excited, bouncing up and down in the back seat like a jack-in-the-box. "Guess what! There's a car following us!"

Jake's hands froze on the steering wheel. He frowned and looked in the rearview mirror. "Where?"

"Behind us, no..." Caitlin twisted around to look. "I can't see it anymore, but it was there."

Jake kept one eye on the mirror, but he didn't see anything suspicious. Nothing but a white station wagon with Florida plates, a pickup truck, and a looming tractor-trailer. The pickup truck passed them as he slowed deliberately. Then the tractor-trailer with a full load of plywood and finally the station wagon.

Margaret saw him look at the fuel gauge. She leaned over and checked. Two-thirds full. They wouldn't need to stop for gas for hours.

She sighed. They could get gas when the needle dropped to a quarter full. In the meantime they could drive like a bat out of hell. Just drive fast enough, and everything would be all right.

"I spilled my fries," Caitlin said in an aggrieved voice. "Now I can't eat them." Grease and catsup was smeared all over the upholstery. "I want an ice cream," she said loudly. When neither Jake nor Margaret answered, she sighed, got out her pencil and notebook. "After I catch Robert and his gang, I'm gonna write my book and maybe I'll go on TV. My picture'll be in all the papers, too."

Why couldn't she be like other kids, Margaret thought. If Caitlin were average, she would be making lists of license plate numbers and states, or how many cows they passed.

Jake downshifted and braked at a traffic light. They saw a string of motels coming up, and Jake pulled off the highway and checked to see if Sandy and Robert were registered. No luck at the first three motels, nor at the fourth. They drove on underneath the blistering sun.

After a while Jake glanced in the mirror again and thought he saw a silver car. He watched it off and on for a time and decided it was gaining on them slowly but surely. There was another exit down the road about forty yards. He turned off and roared down the exit ramp. In the distance there came the whistle of a train.

Two left turns in succession, then a right, and they were a good two miles past the highway, coming up to a grade crossing. No gates to drop down and block passage over the tracks; nothing more than tired, peeling white crossing signs marked the tracks. The railroad was raised several feet to get above the low and often wet countryside.

The whistle screamed again. Jake braked, slamming his foot too hard, and Caitlin was pitched forward against her seat belt in back. The notebook and pencil went flying.

They stared down the track. The train was whipping toward them. They'd never make it if they tried to beat it across the tracks.

The engineer grinned down at them and waved at Caitlin. Jake pounded on the wheel in frustration while Caitlin poked her head out the side window and waved enthusiastically at the train crew. "Hi," she yelled.

"Will you please sit down," Margaret muttered in a low voice.

The train was long, carrying lumber stacked neatly. Margaret had grown up in rural Massachusetts and had seen enough freight trains to know what went on.

Sometimes the wood on trains like this was stacked so badly that it would shift and slide off, which meant the train had to stop while the crew adjusted the load. Since it wasn't their wood, the crew usually just heaved it over the side, that being considerably easier than restacking. But whatever. It meant time. Time while the train was stopped, blocking the grade crossing.

Oh God, don't let anything fall off that train, she prayed.

Caitlin plopped down again. "This seat's awful small," she complained. "And it's hot, too. My legs are sticking to the plastic. How come they didn't make the seats bigger?"

"Because the car wasn't built that way," Jake told her.

Jake looked through the rearview mirror. Nothing to see but empty road. Right next to the road was a falling-in, unpainted frame house. It had been years, he thought, since anyone had put any energy into the collapsing, gray frame house. The windows were long gone, the front porch sagged. An old refrigerator and a broken space heater decorated the doorway.

A few hundred yards to the west were several old barns and a shed. No one moved near them. No engines droned. No voices broke the hot still air. Tire marks had worn away the grass in the front yard of the gray house, but there was no car parked there now. Deep pine woods ringed the back of the farm.

Beside him, Margaret sighed and lifted the hair off her neck. She took a deep breath, sucking in the hot, humid air. If anything, she thought morosely, the train was slowing, swaying. She tried to figure out if the wood stacks were shifting.

Jake smiled reassuringly and glanced back into the mirror. He didn't see a car.

Margaret gripped her hands in her lap and prayed. *Don't let that car find us.* Not while the train's blocking the crossing. She looked out the back window and saw weeds in the front yard of a nearby house moving in the hot wind. What if the driver of that car had a gun, she thought. If he drove up, they would be trapped like sitting ducks.

"Seventy-seven freight cars," Caitlin said proudly, writing it down in her notebook. "I counted."

The caboose, a blue one, trundled across the track, and Jake gunned the accelerator and charged across. In the rearview mirror he caught a glimpse of a silver-gray car just coming around the bend in the road near the unpainted frame house.

The wind that came in the window cooled his sweaty forehead. He floored the accelerator, trying not to swerve, trying to ignore the gleaming silver car coming up fast behind them.

When they reached the highway, no one would change lanes to let them on. Jake had to wait, the motor idling, while three cars and a pickup truck whizzed by. Then he pulled into the traffic lane and accelerated. Out of the corner of his eye he saw the silver car pull onto the highway behind him.

Margaret threw a look in the back seat. Caitlin was so busy writing in her notebook she didn't notice what was going on. She wished she could be calm, but she couldn't forget the way her lungs had ached, starving for air during that murderous attack in the pool. The look of the last air bubbles floating upward and hands strangling her . . .

Jake sighed at the look on her face and said, "Don't think about things we can't control, honey. We'll get there, somehow."

Margaret swallowed a silent sob and stared out the window. There was no way they would make it in time. They had to stop along the way in each and every motel until they found Sandy and Robert. She was sure the silver car would follow along behind, like a huge cat stalking its prey.

Chapter Fourteen

Caitlin was reading a brochure about alligator farms. "It says they eat everything. They've found lots of stuff in their stomachs. Jars of pickles, gold balls... dog collars. It says here one ate a poodle and another got a retriever that went into a canal to fetch a ball for its owner. One time and he was gone, *whump,* ball and all. They taste chewy—sort of like chicken and fish. Alligators, I mean, not dogs." She leaned forward and spoke in Jake's ear. "Could we stop and try a gatorburger?"

He glanced in the rearview mirror and said, "No," almost absentmindedly. He was too busy wondering how many motels they would have to check before they came across Sandy and Robert.

And there was the matter of the silver car following them. He thought of waving down a police car. But he would say someone was following them, and of course there'd be no car around.

They came up to a rest stop. It was a collection of motels and restaurants at an enormous highway interchange. He got out and checked all the motels with no luck. Still no trace of them.

Margaret looked at the map. "This is Route 17, it's a more direct route south. They might have taken it." He nodded, and they turned onto Route 17. They asked in the next three or four motels, but no one had seen or heard of a Mr. and Mrs. Robert Schuyler. They passed a large lake on the left, then the highway traveled past a river flowing quietly westward toward the Gulf of Mexico.

Caitlin didn't seem worried anymore about her lack of gatorburgers. She wasn't even writing in her notebook. She was staring tiredly out the side window at the cloudless sky.

They'd been driving for hours now. Time had ceased. The sun baked away at the landscape, and it was an effort for Jake to exert himself in that fierce light. The dazzle from the highway was blinding. By five o'clock, both the earth and sky seemed absolutely white.

He looked in the mirror again. Dammit, the silver car was there again. He thought they'd lost it at the last motel.

Wearily they continued down the highway. The air in the car was stifling. The gas gauge read one-quarter full. Soon they would have to stop for gas. He began to look for a station and for another fast-food place.

By six o'clock the gas gauge read below one-eighth, and the sun was still beating down on the car. Margaret was wilting in the front seat, and Jake's hands were so wet with sweat he could hardly hold on to the wheel. Thick spongy waves of heat surged through the open windows every time they came to a stoplight.

Jake knew he was watching the mirror more than the road now. The silver-gray car mesmerized him.

The sun glinted off its radiator and darkened wind-shield. He tried to make out what the driver looked like, if it was a man or a woman, but all he could see was the shape of a human head.

What the hell was he going to do? How could he protect both Margaret and Caitlin? What would happen when the sun went down and it got dark? He had a terrible premonition that that was what the driver of the silver car was waiting for. Once the sun set, he would move in for the kill.

Margaret groaned and wiped her face with the back of her hand. She was so tired and hot. Her bones felt like they were softening, melting in this awful heat. Her eyes felt sore and red in the dazzling glare of the lowering sun. She'd lost track of the white line in the road, lost track of time, the hours they'd been driving.

As the dusk of evening drew on, the temperature became cooler, and Caitlin got tired of the awkward posture she'd had to assume to stare out the window with her seat belt still securely fastened. Once more she got out her notebook and worked on a list. It was about Robert and what the police would do to him once he was arrested.

1. they cold make him eat katerpilers till his stomach bustid.

2. throw him off the highest building in Boston without him wearing a parashoot.

3. take his tonsuls out without anastheetik.

"I'm hungry," Caitlin complained. "If I don't eat soon, I'll probably have to go to the hospital."

"All right," Jake replied grimly. "There's a place up ahead. We'll stop there." They pulled in and Margaret got out and took Caitlin inside. She paid for hamburgers and fries and sodas, then took Caitlin to the bathroom. When Caitlin had finished washing her hands, they went back to the car. Jake opened the door for them. Margaret balanced the tray gingerly as she handed a hamburger and a soda into the back seat.

"Gosh, I'm starved," Caitlin said as she took the food and ripped the wrapping from the hamburger.

Margaret got into the front seat. Jake munched on his hamburger as he started up the car. "Aren't you eating?" he asked.

"No." She shook her head. "I got a hamburger for myself, but now the thought of food makes me feel awful."

"You ought to eat," he told her as they pulled into a nearby gas station. "It won't do Sandy any good if you go hungry." Reluctantly she opened up a hamburger and tried to eat.

"Damn," Jake muttered. A sign said out of gas.

And across the street the silver car waited patiently, its motor idling softly. Margaret could see motes of fog dancing in its headlights. They started up the car again and backtracked to the highway. So did the silver car. Jake got the rented car up to seventy and they roared down the road. The rear lights of the cars going fifty-five materialized so fast he couldn't estimate distances. He dropped back to sixty.

The headlights of the silver car crept closer. It was eight o'clock now and dark as the inside of a tomb. ake was so tired he could hardly drive. Unwillingly he recognized they would have to find another gas station, and right away.

Imperceptibly his foot pressed down harder and the car shot forward. He swung the car inland, away from the coast with its spectacular views of the Gulf of Mexico foaming in the purplish dusk. The highway wound westward again, and they reached Marcos Island.

He didn't see any of the island's beauty. His lean face tightened with fury, a muscle working in his jaw. He stared at the glowing headlights in the mirror for the hundredth time. Robert was connected to that silver car—he would bet his life on it.

They were in deadly danger and Jake couldn't do a thing about it. Sweat prickled his forehead. They needed time to find Sandy. He began to calculate with icy fury just what their chances were. They'd covered all the likely motels and turned up nothing. One more motel to go, the Yacht Club Inn and Restaurant. He would go inside, see if they were registered, then, no matter what, he would drive to the nearest police station and see if the state cops could help. He didn't know what else to do. He had a feeling they'd just about used up the last of their nine lives.

Jake saw the sign for the Yacht Club Inn and pulled off the highway. When they reached the motel and parked the car, Margaret got out. No cars had turned in behind them.

"Is Mom here?" Caitlin yawned and looked around.

"We're going to find out." Margaret helped her out of the back seat. Jake put his arm around Margaret's shoulders and they walked toward the entrance. Water splashed in a stone fountain by an elaborate staircase leading to a terrace for outside dining.

Margaret slowed as she glanced toward the restaurant. "Let's check the restaurant first. If they're registered here, maybe they're still eating."

At the top of the stairs they scanned the seated diners. At first no one seemed to resemble Sandy and Robert, then Margaret saw a blond woman touching her wineglass to that of her companion. She laughed, a low, delicious chuckle, and Margaret grabbed Jake's sleeve. *"That's Sandy, and she's all right!"*

Caitlin darted through the scattered tables. "Mommy!"

Startled, Sandy turned her head and Robert stood up, his attention focused on the man walking behind Margaret.

A grin spread across Sandy's pale face. "Wha...at are you doing here?" Scooping Caitlin into her arms, she glanced at Margaret. "How did you find us?"

"It's a long story." Margaret kissed her. "Are you okay?"

"Robert's taking good care of me..." Sandy's smile faded. "But this bug won't quit."

He put his hand on her shoulder. "Darling, this is Jake McCall." He hesitated, then said with a sheepish grin, "The truth is I was married to Jake's sister some years ago. He's my former brother-in-law."

Sandy stared, but didn't seem to know what to say. Finally she whispered, "You were...married before?"

He squeezed her shoulder. "It was tragic, darling. She died of asthma, a terribly sad thing. Which is why I never told you."

She frowned and put down her wineglass. "Why don't we go back to the room. I . . . I don't know what to say." She got up, pushing her chair back.

Jake said grimly, "We're coming, too. Margaret and I have a few things to discuss with you."

Sandy shrugged and, holding an uncharacteristically subdued Caitlin by the hand, led them down the steps and around the back of the motel to their room.

Robert's face was shiny with sweat, and he had some trouble getting the key in the door lock. Finally it clicked open, and they went inside. Behind them the door didn't quite swing shut.

Sandy switched on the bureau lamp. A brown leather suitcase lay beside it. Robert's probably, Jake thought grimly. He wondered what it contained. Maybe, just maybe there might be some proof in that suitcase they could use.

He took another look at the suitcase. It wasn't locked.

"I'd like to tell you a story about money and murder," Jake said quietly.

Sandy sat down on the bed with a bewildered look on her face. "I don't understand. . . ."

Jake shrugged and put his hand on the suitcase. "Robert inherited a trust fund when my sister died."

Robert's eyes narrowed to blue-white ice chips. "Hey, that was three years ago. What the hell's gotten into you?"

"I'll bet you played the stock market and lost. Or was it real estate that went bust?" Robert's face went red, the line of his mouth grim, and Jake knew his shot had struck home. "What's in the suitcase? Pills you are using to poison Sandy?"

Margaret grabbed Caitlin and dragged her to the bathroom. "Stay in there," she told her. "Don't come out."

"But I want to read my clues." Caitlin took out her notebook and flipped the pages. "I can tell Mom about Madame Zorina and how I'm gonna save everyone."

"Not now!" Margaret hissed. "Stay here and be quiet." She turned around as Jake flipped open the suitcase. Right on top was a plastic bag full of pill bottles.

"My allergy medicine. No big deal." Robert took a step toward the suitcase. Light winked off his snake's head belt buckle.

Jake picked up the plastic bag. The bottles inside rattled eerily in the sudden silence. "Let's have this analyzed. What do you think we'll find...barbiturates? Downers, tranquilizers?"

Robert took another step toward the suitcase. His face was angry, his eyes glittered with fury. "The joke's gone far enough. It's not funny."

"Betsy's death wasn't funny. You killed her, you bastard! Then you ran through her money and looked around for another victim." Jake threw the bag of pills back in the suitcase. "You and your girlfriend, Polly Merrill...now Mrs. Knox. She saw the old lady's will, and you spent months romancing the wrong niece."

Sandy stared at both men, her face pale. "What's he talking about...*girlfriend...killing? Robert, please...what does he mean?*"

"Sandy," Jake tried to say as calmly as possible, "Polly Knox knew who you were before you rented her house." Jake stopped a minute, and then went on,

"Since Mrs. Knox is a nurse—and I use the term loosely—she was employed by your aunt to take care of her before she died. And she did more than nursing. Somehow she got hold of your aunt's will and found out about a niece who would inherit lots of money.

"She only made one mistake," Jake said, shrugging his wide shoulders. "The name of the niece who inherited everything."

"I talked to your doctor in Vermont, Sandy. He never prescribed antibiotics for you," Margaret said.

"No one'll believe any of it." Robert's noisy breathing seemed to fill the room like a rushing wind, yet the silence was so complete the click of the air conditioner coming on was perfectly audible. He flexed his fists.

Sandy moved out of his reach and picked up the phone. "I think . . . I want to call . . ."

Robert twisted his mouth into a parody of a smile. "Honey, you don't believe this, do you? Hey, it's a damn lie. Wait a second, I love you. Listen, Margaret's had it in for me ever since I broke our engagement. She's jealous."

Jake took hold of Robert's arm and shoved him toward the door. "It's over. You're finished." In a blur, pivoting angrily, Robert shrugged off Jake's arm and threw a punch, knocking him backward into the bureau. The lamp crashed over, the shade tilting crazily.

Jake got up, swaying dizzily.

A letter opener lay by the fallen lamp. Robert grabbed it, striking in a blur of speed, swinging the blade in Jake's face. Jake managed to turn partly away from the blow, but the blade tore along the side of his head, drawing blood. He sagged, dazed, dropping to his knees.

Margaret backed away, yelling desperately to Sandy who stood frozen by the end of the bed. "Get the police! For God's sake, Sandy, move!" An icy shiver ran up her spine at the numb, disbelieving look on her sister's face.

Robert lunged forward. "Damn, I should have taken care of you a long time ago!" He took Margaret down, screaming and kicking, a tangle of arms and legs. His lips twisted into a grisly smile. "I'm going to take my time with you and make you suffer first before I kill you!"

Caitlin peered out the crack in the bathroom door, then shrank back in the shadows as a blond-haired woman walked silently through the half-open motel room door... and reached into her purse, pulling out a gun. "It's all right. I'm here, Robert, and I'll blow the head off anyone who tries anything."

Caitlin stared from the darkness of the bathroom. The woman smiled and thumbed two tiny levers on the gun. Caitlin wondered what a master detective would do in a situation like this. Her mother wasn't calling the police, she was still frozen, staring blank-eyed.

Very carefully Caitlin slipped out of the bathroom. The woman didn't see her, her back was turned, and she was focused on Robert who was getting off Margaret.

Robert stood and composed himself. "A nasty car accident is in order. We'll find a deserted side road and set the car on fire. That'll take care of things nicely."

Caitlin crept silently out the motel room door. Outside was a planter with flowers and a large rock. *If anyone's going to save everyone, it's got to be me,* she thought grimly. She picked up the rock and went to look in the window.

Robert was hitting Jake in the face, and her mother was shaking as if she couldn't believe her eyes. The woman with the gun was pointing it at Margaret, lining up the sight.

Caitlin threw the rock as hard as she could; the window smashed and glass flew, hitting the woman. She screamed and dropped the gun. Margaret grabbed it, pointing it with jittery hands at Robert and the woman who was cradling her wrist as if it were broken. "Don't move, I'll shoot!"

"It's okay, Mom, I fixed Robert." Caitlin ran and put her arms around her mother. She stared at the blond woman; somehow she looked familiar. Then she put two and two together. Wow, Mrs. Knox wasn't dead after all! Robert hadn't killed her and thrown her in the quarry.

Robert glared at Polly. "This is your fault, dammit! Didn't you see the kid at your back?"

She winced as if he'd struck her. "You got us into this mess with your greed. First it was Wanda Marshall you had to marry six years ago. 'A little extra digitalis would take care of her bad heart,' you said. 'The doctors won't suspect a thing.' I was satisfied with her money. But no, you had to get your hands on Betsy McCall's money. The law of averages caught up with us. 'Just one more,' you said. So you married this one, and now my wrist is broken and look what it got us—jail!"

Robert glared furiously, sweat gleaming on his handsome face. "You lying bitch, who killed Martha

Knox? And that fool husband of hers? You're the one who injected a syringeful of air into the old geezer."

Beside herself with anger and pain, Polly raged on. "I married you nine years ago for better or worse. We didn't need all this money. I went along with what you wanted because I loved you."

"Shut up," he snarled. "Your hands are as bloody as mine. You couldn't just pay off Vern Boyce. No, you had to kill him. So why didn't you finish off Margaret in the pool? It should have been a piece of cake." He noticed Margaret's hands holding the gun were shaking, and he grinned.

"One wrong move and I'll shoot," Margaret said weakly.

Robert moved toward her. He was less than eight feet away. "Looks like you'd better say your prayers."

The snake's eyes glittered at his waist, and Margaret shuddered. Madame Zorina's warning about the silver serpent.

Chapter Fifteen

She pulled the trigger. Nothing happened. She pulled it again. Still nothing. Dazed and bloody, Jake struggled to his feet, realizing she'd forgotten to jack a bullet into the chamber. "Margaret, pump a bullet into the chamber!"

She bit her lip and fumbled desperately with the gun, then squeezed off a shot just as Robert laughed . . . and lunged at her like a demon from hell.

The sound of the shot filled the room. It echoed off the walls and reverberated in the windows. Robert went down, groaning, a wet red stain spreading down his trouser leg.

"Wow!" Caitlin was round-eyed. She took out her pencil and began scribbling in her notebook.

Margaret couldn't move. She'd actually fired a gun. She felt sick to her stomach, but kept the gun pointed at Robert and Polly.

Behind her Sandy hung up the phone. "The police are on the way. They'll be here any minute."

Carefully Jake removed the gun from Margaret's trembling fingers. "Let me hold that, Annie Oakley.

I'll keep an eye on them." He put an arm around her. "Okay?"

She nodded numbly, staring at the blond woman. There was something about her. And then she knew. Polly Knox was Violet Chadwick! The same woman who'd come to the house in Vermont, saying she was an old friend.

She'd worn dark makeup to disguise the contours of her face, dark glasses and a wig. High heels had added height.

"Why didn't you drown last night?" Polly hissed. "You and your sister were fools to think Robert ever loved you. He's mine!" Her voice dripped venom.

Jake jerked the gun at her. "That's enough. You can tell your story to the police."

"I should have climbed down the mountain and put a bullet through you when I had the chance," Polly snarled. "Stirring up trouble, asking questions. Like Vern Boyce, nosing around once too often, blackmailing me. You should have ended up like him. Dead."

Margaret shivered and turned her face into Jake's shoulder. He kissed her hair. "It's okay now. It's all over."

JAKE SHOOK HIS HEAD, watching the police load Robert and Polly into the back of a cruiser. Polly had had a bout of wild hysterics as they handcuffed her. She was calm now, but her eyes were wild, her mouth creased with hate.

"Vern Boyce really must have been putting the arm on her," he said with a tired sigh. "He must have had suspicions about Wendell Knox's death, then recognized Polly Knox in town at the toy shop when she was supposed to be in Europe. He blackmailed her, but she wouldn't play that game.''

Margaret leaned on his shoulder. ''And with his drinking, he was bound to let something slip. She had to get rid of him.''

''Caitlin was right all along.'' He bent down and kissed her hair. ''Polly followed us on the plane, and when you were alone by the pool, she tried to kill you.''

''I managed to fight her off until she heard people coming and let me go, thinking I was dead.'' Margaret shuddered a little.

He dropped another kiss on her hair and held her close. ''Thank God, you weren't.''

With the departure of the police, things were still in an uproar. Sandy's room was cordoned off, the scene of a crime. Jake led Sandy, Caitlin, and Margaret back to the main lobby and rented a couple of rooms for the night.

Sandy sat in a chair in an alcove just off the lobby. She turned as Margaret came in. She was calm, but her face was smudged with tears. Margaret sat down and gave her a cup of coffee. ''Compliments of the management. Don't worry about Caitlin. She's safe and sound with Jake. There's a game room next door.''

Sandy smiled. ''He seems very nice. Thank him for me, will you? Caitlin—''

''Is having the time of her life, making up rules as she goes. Don't worry,'' Margaret said.

''How could I have been so blind?'' Tears glittered in Sandy's eyes. ''All that time...everything was a *lie*.''

"He was an expert, a pathological liar, smooth as silk." Margaret shrugged sadly. "He fooled a lot of women, including me."

"You saved my life," Sandy whispered, her voice breaking. She drew a shaky breath and wiped her cheeks with the back of her hand. "My God, he poisoned me for months. I kept getting weaker and weaker... I never guessed."

Margaret reached over and hugged her for a long time. "Hush, it's all over now. He can't hurt you anymore."

At last Sandy smiled a little. "I still don't know how you and Jake figured out what Robert and Polly Knox were up to. Caitlin said something about... a fortune-teller and a full moon and a snake." She looked puzzled. "What sent you down here just in time? Straight out of the blue like that? Was it Jake? Did he know or suspect Robert?"

Margaret's lips quirked into a grin. She shook her head. "You'll never believe me."

"Try me."

"It was Caitlin and a fortune-teller up in Rochester. Somehow the woman had real powers, and she tuned in on Caitlin."

"You're right. I don't believe it." Sandy shook her head.

"I'll let Caitlin fill you in on the details, especially the part where she's the heroine."

"Which, knowing my daughter, is the most important part." Sandy sighed and shook her head. "She's something else, my Caitlin."

"She's a darling. I wouldn't change a hair on her head." Margaret hugged Sandy once more. "But am

I ever glad she's yours, not mine. She's—'' She searched for the words, but Sandy merely smiled and found them for her.

"Enough to drive a person straight up a wall."

A HALF HOUR LATER Margaret tucked Caitlin in for the night. "I wish I'd hit her in the head and killed her dead," Caitlin remarked. "Mrs. Knox was really wicked, wasn't she?" Margaret nodded, and Caitlin went on with another yawn, "She was going to kill you, just like Madame Zorina said. And I saved everyone."

"That's right." Margaret brushed the hair off her niece's forehead and dropped a kiss on her nose. "Thank you, honey."

Caitlin frowned and hitched herself up in bed. "One thing Madame Zorina was wrong about. She said a snake was gonna get you, a silver one. But there wasn't any snake."

Margaret nodded. "Madame Zorina was right about that, too. Robert was wearing a belt with a silver buckle, shaped like a snake's head."

"Oh, yeah, I 'member I saw it." In a lurid flash Caitlin saw it again in her mind. Robert holding his bleeding leg, the light winking off his green-eyed belt buckle. "Wow!" She thought a minute, then gave Margaret a shrewd look. "So now we can go to Disneyworld. Mom's in the shower, but she said the police will want to talk to us for a few days. And if she's busy, then you and Jake can take me, right?"

"Okay, it's a deal," Margaret promised with a broad smile. "Know something funny?"

"What?" Caitlin asked sleepily.

"Your Mom says I was a lot like you when I was seven."

"Did you save people from getting killed by bad guys?"

Margaret shook her head. "Not quite. But I jumped off a shed roof, pretending I was Superman. I wore a towel on my back." She grinned. "I really thought I could fly."

Caitlin considered this for a second, then frowned. "You couldn't fly?"

"No, I broke my ankle and couldn't swim for a whole summer. But you know what?"

"What?" Caitlin looked puzzled.

"In a way you were Superman tonight. You were flying."

"Ackshully, I'm a master detective." Caitlin corrected her with a sleepy yawn.

"Yes, you are, and I love you very much." Margaret hugged her tight, kissed her and turned off the light. As she left the room, Jake took her in his arms.

He cocked a quizzical eyebrow down at her. "What was that all about?"

She grinned and shook her head. "Superman was just having a chat with the great master detective."

"You've got me completely confused. Superman? I don't know..."

"It's a long story, part of my checkered past involving a shed roof, a towel and my unshakable belief that I could fly."

His eyes crinkled with laughter. "I see. In that case, how would Superman like to move in with me? We could get married."

"My apartment's bigger, so you're moving in with me. Besides, I'm not sure I want to go to Australia." She reached up and brushed his lips with hers. "I like Boston. It's got swan boats, the Bruins and the Celtics. I forgot to tell you, when I bleed, it's Celtic green. I'm a fanatic basketball fan. They don't play basketball in Australia, do they?"

"I don't know." A gleam warmed his gray-blue eyes. "I only know I love you to distraction, from the first moment we met. You opened the door, and I was a goner."

"Actually, Caitlin opened the door."

The corners of his mouth turned up. "I stand corrected."

"That's okay, Caitlin's enough to confuse anyone." She smiled up at him. "Now where are we going to live?"

"I don't know," he admitted with an irresistible crooked grin. "I've got a place in New Haven where I hang my hat, and a cabin in Maine. We can find a place to put you."

Her toes curled and her heart melted and she knew she'd live anywhere as long as he was there, too.

"Want to guess what I like?" he teased.

"No, you tell me," she said, softly kissing his lean jaw.

"LOOK AT THIS!" Margaret exclaimed three months later as she was sorting through replies to their wedding invitations. There was a large postcard with a picture of an Atlantic City casino among the small white envelopes.

Jake snatched it out of her fingers and turned it over, whistling in surprise. "Of all people, our favorite fortune-teller, the one and only Madame Zorina!"

Margaret slid her arms around him and kissed his mouth. "What does she say?"

He took time out for another kiss, then read the card aloud.

Dear Margaret and Jake,
Naturally you are getting married. Didn't I tell you your fates were entwined? Relieved all is well and that terrible threat has been removed. So, Robert Schuyler was the serpent, just as I foretold! And that woman, striking the night of the full moon, trying to drown you! I read the entire account in the newspapers. Caitlin, of course, saved your lives, it all happened as I said it would. The little girl is headed for great things. Sorry to say I will not be able to attend your wedding. I have been barred from the Atlantic City casinos. Apparently they resented my winning so much of their money! I plan to be in Las Vegas for the next few weeks, and after that, Monte Carlo! My aura is bright and the moon is in Saturn. I read the Tarot, and the cards looked very promising. Adding them all, I got a total of sixty-six, and the card ruling my sign was the Wheel of Fortune! My good luck continues! I shall let nature and the Fates take their course.

Affectionately, Madame Zorina.

Jake plucked the card from her fingers and read it. "Well, looks like she won the jackpot."

Sliding her arms about him, Margaret kissed him on the mouth. "Mmm, know what I think?" she said, slightly light-headed from his closeness.

"What?" Jake's arms tightened around her, and the postcard fell to the floor.

After an interval she laid her head on his shoulder and smiled. "We're the ones who hit the jackpot." Her breath caught in her throat at the look of love she saw in his eyes. Then further discussion of Madame Zorina and jackpots became nonessential as Margaret gave herself up to the delights of Jake's warm, crushing embrace; and the glow of love surrounded them both like a golden halo.

ROMANCE IS A YEARLONG EVENT!

Celebrate the most romantic day of the year with MY VALENTINE! (February)

CRYSTAL CREEK
When you come for a visit Texas-style, you won't want to leave! (March)

Celebrate the joy, excitement and adjustment that comes with being JUST MARRIED! (April)

Go back in time and discover the West as it was meant to be . . . UNTAMED—Maverick Hearts! (July)

LINGERING SHADOWS
New York Times bestselling author Penny Jordan brings you her latest blockbuster. Don't miss it! (August)

BACK BY POPULAR DEMAND!!!
Calloway Corners, involving stories of four sisters coping with family, business and romance! (September)

FRIENDS, FAMILIES, LOVERS
Join us for these heartwarming love stories that evoke memories of family and friends. (October)

Capture the magic and romance of Christmas past with HARLEQUIN HISTORICAL CHRISTMAS STORIES! (November)

WATCH FOR FURTHER DETAILS IN ALL HARLEQUIN BOOKS!

CALEND

Take 4 bestselling love stories FREE

Plus get a FREE surprise gift!

HARLEQUIN®

my
Valentine

1993

The most romantic day of the year is here! Escape into the exquisite world of love with MY VALENTINE 1993. What better way to celebrate Valentine's Day than with this very romantic, sensuous collection of four original short stories, written by some of Harlequin's most popular authors.

ANNE STUART
JUDITH ARNOLD
ANNE McALLISTER
LINDA RANDALL WISDOM

THIS VALENTINE'S DAY, DISCOVER ROMANCE WITH MY VALENTINE 1993

Available in February wherever Harlequin Books are sold.   VAL93

HARLEQUIN · HISTORICAL ·

CHRISTMAS

·STORIES·1992·

Capture the magic and romance of Christmas in the 1800s with HARLEQUIN HISTORICAL CHRISTMAS STORIES 1992, a collection of three stories by celebrated historical authors. The perfect Christmas gift!

Don't miss these heartwarming stories, available in November wherever Harlequin books are sold:

MISS MONTRACHET REQUESTS by Maura Seger
CHRISTMAS BOUNTY by Erin Yorke
A PROMISE KEPT by Bronwyn Williams

Plus, as an added bonus, you can receive a FREE keepsake Christmas ornament. Just collect four proofs of purchase from any November or December 1992 Harlequin or Silhouette series novels, or from any Harlequin or Silhouette Christmas collection, and receive a beautiful dated brass Christmas candle ornament.

Mail this certificate along with four (4) proof-of-purchase coupons plus $1.50 postage and handling (check or money order—do not send cash), payable to Harlequin Books, to: **In the U.S.**: P.O. Box 9057, Buffalo, NY 14269-9057; **In Canada**: P.O. Box 622, Fort Erie, Ontario, L2A 5X3.